A ROBUST, FULL-BODIED MYSTERY

"The finale, staged in a storage room filled with empty kegs, with Spraggue pitted against a megalomaniac killer, is a real thriller."

Publishers Weekly

"A heady blend of wine and murder, full of wine tastings, harvest talk, unlikeable wine critics, star winemakers and winery sell-outs to conglomerates...a polished production...it has an attractive flavor and definite charm. We'd rate it 16/20 and ready to enjoy now."

Food & Wine

"Thanks to the intriguing wine-biz detail and a hero with panache: lively, solid mystery-entertainment."

The Kirkus Reviews

"A solid, traditional mystery, with fairly planted clues, and a good pace."

Library Journal

BITTER FINISH

Linda Barnes

FAWCETT CREST • NEW YORK

AUTHOR'S NOTE

That the Napa Valley produces some of the finest wines in
the world today is unassailable fact. As for the rest, this is a
work of fiction. Holloway Hills, Landover Valley, and Leider
Vineyards exist only in the author's imagination. All char-
acters are fictitious, and any resemblance to actual persons,
living or dead, is purely coincidental.

A Fawcett Crest Book
Published by Ballantine Books
Copyright © 1983 by Linda Appelblatt Barnes

Library of Congress Catalog Card Number: 82-17040

ISBN 0-449-20690-4

This edition published by arrangement with St. Martin's Press

Manufactured in the United States of America

First Ballantine Books Edition: June 1985

To Richard

ACKNOWLEDGMENT

I am grateful to Phillip E. Stewart, the sheriff of Napa County; Gayle Keller, the editor of *Vintage-wise*; the staff of the Winecellar of Silene; and the staff of the Brookline Liquor Mart for answering my many questions concerning the history and lore of the Napa Valley and the production of wine.

Steven Appelblatt, Richard Barnes, and James Morrow commented on this book in its earlier stages—I thank them.

1

"KNEE PADS?"

"Check."

"Elbow pads?"

"Check."

"Extra flannel stuffed in your long johns?"

"Feels like ten yards of it." Michael Vincent Spraggue III stared impatiently at the beefy man some ten feet below and cautiously removed his hand from a rickety one-by-three some carpenter had thoughtfully installed as a guardrail. "Strapped, taped, and padded. Just stick a gag in my mouth so I won't have to say this god-awful line when I fall."

"Can't be too careful," the stuntman said drily. "Especially with one of our stars. You ready?"

Spraggue wiped his sweaty palms off on his corduroy pants. From where he stood, on a rough-boarded five-foot-square platform at the top of a built-for-the occasion flight of wooden stairs, he could look down on the basketball hoops at either end of the old YMCA gym on Huntington Avenue. The distant floor was reassuringly

1

padded with tumbling mats. The steps weren't. He tried not to think about slivers.

He seemed taller than the six feet one claimed on his résumé, too thin for his height. His shoulders were broad enough, but when he took off his shirt every rib stuck out like a spoke. Women tried to feed him; stuntmen recommended extra padding.

He ran the back of his hand across his forehead and hoped the beads of fear-sweat weren't too visible. His face was a careful blank, remarkable more for its mobility than any uniqueness of feature. Studying it in repose, emptied of emotion, one could note the slight asymmetry that accounted for the marked differences in left and right profiles. His eyes were an odd pale golden-tawny color that defied driver's license description. When asked, he called them brown.

"I said, you ready?"

"Yeah," Spraggue said reluctantly.

"Okay. No fall this time. Just a nice easy roll down the steps."

"You sure you don't want to count it out? Slowly?"

"It's *only* ten steps. For a movie. You won't have to do it every night on Broadway."

"Still," Spraggue said, lying down at an angle, "I'd really hate to wind up with any critical portion of my anatomy in a sling."

"That's why I'm here: to make sure you don't."

Spraggue wriggled backward so that his right hip rested on the very edge of the platform, then eased himself down until his shoulder met the first step. He kept a firm hold on the handrail and glanced below. The platform suddenly seemed to shoot up like an elevator. The foot of the stairs turned into a distant runway. The phone jangled.

He looked up hopefully.

The stuntman frowned. "Three, two, one, *now*."

Spraggue closed his eyes, released his grip finger by finger, and shoved off with his right foot.

"Relax, dammit! Protect your head. Hit on your butt and your thighs. Roll with it!" Spraggue gritted his teeth and thought he could do without the play-by-play. "Now roll when you land. Roll! Good!"

He lay winded, but exhilarated, on the mat. It wasn't that much different from his first high dive. He wiggled his fingers and toes, stretched each extremity independently. No broken bones.

Muted footsteps approached, vibrating the floorboards. "Mr. Spraggue?"

The stuntman must have pointed down at him. Spraggue turned his head and winced. One muscle, on the left side of his neck, hadn't enjoyed the fall.

"Telephone. Says its urgent."

He got slowly to his feet, marched into the hallway without limping, and snatched the receiver off the hook.

"Spraggue?"

How many months since he'd heard that gravelly voice? His mouth spread into a slow smile. "Holloway," he said.

"Right the first time."

"How are you?"

"It's about Lenny."

"God, Kate. Again?"

The stuntman lumbered heavily across the hall, gestured up at the clock. Spraggue nodded; if he didn't want any more "star" razz, he'd better keep the call short.

"Look, I'm busy. Are you home?"

"I'm at the Napa County Sheriff's Office."

"Can I call you?—Wait." He turned his back on the stuntman, lowered his voice. "What the hell are you doing there?"

"Having my civil rights violated. It took me forever to get a hold of you, and don't you dare say you'll call me back!"

"What's going on?"

"Lenny's missing."

"Who'd miss him?"

"*We* would, dammit!" Her voice dropped. "Michael, it's *harvest*. The crush is going full tilt. We *need* him."

"Okay," Spraggue said soothingly, glancing at the stuntman's impatient face. "Okay. So Lenny's flown."

"Gone. For three days. I called the police this morning. And the hospitals. Everyone I could think of. No winemaker would just run off in the middle of the harvest."

"And?" \

"Nothing. Then after lunch, a squad car pulled up in front of the winery. This cop asked me to—to identify someone, if I could. I didn't know—I went with him."

"Where?"

"Some funeral home. I don't know....Christ, Michael, it was awful."

"Lenny? Car accident?"

He heard a long shuddering sigh and then the customary firmness crept back into Kate Holloway's voice. "I don't know who it was. But it couldn't have been a car crash. Even seventy miles an hour into a bridge abutment wouldn't do that to a man."

"Do what?"

"It made me throw up in front of a goddamned deputy sheriff. You know how long it's been since I've gotten sick like that? Maybe when I was five. And then, I made it to the bathroom..."

"Take it easy."

"It was like he'd fallen off a ten-story building and landed smack on his head. Almost nothing left. And he wanted me to identify that... that thing... as Lenny."

"Kate, go home. Get in the tub. Open a bottle of—"

"Why in hell do you think I'm calling you? For sympathy? They're not about to let me go home and soak in the bubbles. I need you here. With Lenny gone...and me in jail...and the grapes coming in by the ton— You've got a lot invested in that winery, and if you get here as soon as you can—"

"Back up. Why won't they let you go home?"

"You must be sleeping, Michael! I call the cops this morning about a missing man, and he turns up dead, practically on my doorstep, and—"

"You don't know it's Lenny."

"I don't know it's not. Maybe you could look at it. I can't. Not again."

4

"Where did they find the body?"

"In that clearing near Mary's Vineyard. With the big rocks and the old rusted-out car we always planned to have towed. In the trunk of the car."

"Shit."

"Exactly."

"That's still no reason for the police to assume you're involved. Christ, from what you read in the Boston papers, Californians slaughter each other for the hell of it every day. Hillside Strangler, Sunset Strip Murderer. The coast is supposed to be psycho-killer haven, isn't it?"

"Maybe the sheriff doesn't read the *Globe*." The phone made a clicking noise. "Look, I've got to hang up. Can you come? Are you working?"

"I've got a film. *Still Waters*. Like the title?"

"Congratulations."

"Hollywood detective crap."

"So why are you doing it?"

Sprague rubbed his shoulders, shrugged painfully. "Actors act."

"Even independently wealthy ones?"

"Yeah. Look, I've got some location shots in Boston Sunday. I'm due in L.A. Thursday. I could—"

"That's a whole week away, Sprague."

"Hang on a minute, Holloway." He covered the mouthpiece with his hand, looked up at the clock: four thirty. "Matt!" he hollered.

The stuntman's lazy footsteps padded across the gym.

"Can you work late tonight?" Sprague asked.

"How late?"

"Late enough to get me ready for the Boston shooting?"

Matt pushed out his thin lips, paused. "That's a lot of punishment." He grinned suddenly. "Still, it's a lot of overtime, too. If you can clear it with the union—"

"I'll take care of it." Sprague put the receiver back to his ear. "Kate, listen. I'll finish up here tonight. There's a ten A.M. flight from Logan. Five hours minus the time-zone change. San Francisco by noon. Napa, a little after

5

one. I'll call the house. If you're not there, I'll go straight to the sheriff's. In Napa?"

"Can't miss it. Right in the middle of town."

"Tomorrow, then."

"Great. Good-bye, darling."

Darling.

"Get a lawyer," Spraggue said quickly.

She'd already hung up. She was always the first to hang up.

"Okay," the stuntman said, "this time we do the stairs with the fall at the top, then we'll add the fight and the punch. And then the two other fights. Those we'll have to choreograph. By the numbers. You'll like that."

Spraggue's right eyebrow shot up. "Do they make thicker knee pads?" he asked.

2

SPRAGGUE DIDN'T EXPECT ANY WELCOMING COMMITTEE at the San Francisco International Airport. He'd already deplaned from a blissfully boring coast-to-coast 747, strolled down miles of featureless corridor, and was tapping his foot in the Hertz line when he glimpsed Philip Leider, gesturing wildly from a hundred yards down the hallway. No one else answered the fat man's frantic semaphores, so Spraggue waved in return.

"Thought I'd missed you," Leider gasped, his bulk heaving with the exertion of moving two hundred and fifty pounds of middle-aged man.

"How are you, Phil?" Spraggue shook hands and gave Leider a chance to catch his breath.

The fat man beamed. "Just fine."

"What are you doing here?"

"I spoke to Kate this morning on the phone from the county jail. Asked if there was any way I could help. It's all over the valley by now, you can imagine. She told me you were on the way, so I volunteered to fetch and carry."

"I could've rented a car." Spraggue dismissed with

7

little regret thoughts of the portable tape recorder he'd brought along, the lines he'd vowed to memorize on the drive to the valley. "You must be up to your eyeballs in grapes at your place—"

"Waste of money, renting cars. Kate's got transport you can use. Luggage?"

Spraggue hefted a carry-on duffel. "Just what you see."

"Good. I'm double-parked. Impossible to find a space."

Spraggue followed Leider's bobbing head out into the pale sunshine. He doubted that Leider had made any attempt to park legally. For such an important winery owner, they ought to reserve a private space. With a doorman.

"To tell you the truth," Leider said, patting the trunk of a deep-red BMW 633 CSi before unlocking it, "I wanted to run down in my new toy. Like it?"

Spraggue nodded appreciatively and Leider opened the passenger door with a flourish. "The small winery owners of Napa have to stick together," he said.

Spraggue prepared for a gut-wrenching journey. It was obvious even before they got to Highway 101 that the fat man was an incompetent driver. He attacked the gearshift with exasperating clumsiness. Spraggue felt sorry for the car.

"Shocking." Leider mumbled the word under his breath.

"Traffic?" Spraggue hazarded. All rotten drivers like someone else to blame.

"Arresting Kate Holloway like that. Like some cheap thug."

"She probably talked back to somebody."

"She would." Leider grimaced. Spraggue wished the man would keep his eyes on the road. "But it *is* ridiculous. The killer'll turn out to be some nut. They're everyplace, especially around here. Those sixties' kids who flocked to the sunshine to find the answers and can't even remember the questions. You see them everywhere: vacant faces hitching rides to nowhere. Scary-looking sad-faced zombies. I don't pick up hitchers any more. And hitchhikers, they're taking a gamble every time they get in a car with a stranger."

"With all those loonies to choose from, suppose the cops picked on Kate?"

"Sheer laziness. She was there on the spot. What could be neater? Our sheriff's an elected official, you know. The Honorable B. Ridley Hughes."

"You sound less than enthusiastic."

"*B* for bonehead. But don't worry. He won't come out unless there's a chance for a lot of favorable publicity. You'll deal with some deputy or other."

"Comforting," Sprague said, clinging to the padded arm rest.

"All this violence," Leider muttered, his stubby fingers drumming the steering wheel. "Crime on the streets, in the movies, on TV—"

A Toyota gave a yelping honk as Leider cut it off with a quick unsignaled lane change.

"On the roads," Sprague said quietly.

The corner of Leider's mouth twitched. "But it's not the *violence* on TV I'm most concerned about. Oh no. It's the damned wine ads. Orson Welles hypnotizing people with that gorgeous voice. 'Wine-tasting' schools. Chic little parties with sophisticated guests all drinking swill!"

Sprague laughed.

"It's serious! They work. Big business is raking it in. Coca-Cola, by God! General Foods! The industry's getting away from us. Small owners are in hot water. Every day you hear about another corporate takeover. Advertising's ruining everything."

"The jug-wine market's booming, agreed. But there's still demand for premium varietals—"

"Your average yokel can't tell Mouton from grape juice. He listens to those shills who tell him McDonald's hamburgers are better than the food he cooks in his own home."

"Not everyone listens."

"Labor and production are both skyrocketing. And now advertising costs! And all those new wineries keep springing up! They're going to saturate the market. The little guys have got to stick together."

How little?" Spraggue asked. "I hear you're getting pretty substantial yourself."

"Personally or professionally?" Leider stared down at his expansive stomach and laughed. The BMW came perilously close to a dirty white van displaying a SAVE THE WHALES bumper sticker. Spraggue resolved not to speak to Leider while he was within five car-lengths of any other vehicle.

Instead he stared out the window at the parched brown hills. This year's drought hadn't been as severe as last year's, but the visitor expecting lush greenery would have been disappointed. The landscape was broken up by fences and power lines, railroad tracks and distant lonely houses. Spraggue read the signs with their Spanish place names, relived past California vacations, nights in Carmel and Monterey with Kate. . . .

The fat man let Spraggue scramble for the 40-cent Carquinez Bridge toll.

He'd met her in England, contriving to fall practically into her lap when the crowded underground jerked to a halt at Sloane Square Station. That had been well over a decade ago, when he was still a student at the Royal Academy of Dramatic Art. She'd been a tourist, and London was just a stopover on the way to Paris. That stopover grew into a two-day fling, then into a week, a month, six months. Even now he had only to catch the scent of a certain perfume in the wake of some passing woman to conjure up Kate as she'd been that first day in the tube . . . that short white skirt against long tanned velvet legs. . . .

Despite the air-conditioning, the car was getting warm. Spraggue cracked the side window down an inch.

After six months she'd moved on to Paris. They wrote letters that scorched the stationery, made wild plans, and met for scattered hurried weekends. Distance had begun to sour their reunions long before Kate met another man. In all the intervening years of anger and friendship, platonic and romantic, they'd never recaptured that initial spark or successfully said good-bye. Their business partnership was only partly the reason.

10

"Good-bye, darling," she'd said before hanging up.

Spraggue turned reluctantly back to the present. He wasn't on his way to the county sheriff's office to rekindle old flames.

Leider, now breezing along at a triumphantly illegal seventy-five miles an hour, flashed Spraggue a cheerful grin. They whizzed around an orange VW bug with six inches to spare, and Spraggue decided to risk a question.

"Have you seen Lenny Brent recently?"

Leider started. The steering wheel jumped in his hands. "Isn't he the one—Isn't Kate in jail for—"

"The corpse hasn't been identified."

"Oh. Well, I haven't seen him since he ran off to Holloway Hills—five, six months ago. You got a damn fine winemaker."

"No hard feelings?"

Leider shrugged, took his hands completely off the wheel. "Brent and I were overdue for a split. He's not the easiest guy to work with."

"He made you some fine wines."

"He *helped*. I'm not exactly a stranger to winemaking."

"No offense."

"None taken. I appreciated Lenny's talent more than his personality. In a lot of ways he was a pain to have around. Agreed?"

"You wouldn't find anyone who'd disagree."

"He gets along with Kate." Leider gave him a sidelong glance and turned off the freeway at First Street. The change in roads meant no change in speed. Not to Leider.

"Kate's not hard to get along with," Spraggue said.

Leider needed silence to negotiate the narrow Napa streets. Spraggue played tourist. Napa had always been a jog to the left on Route 29 for him, never a destination.

The red BMW pulled up sharply in front of a small shop. The sign overhead proclaimed BAIL BONDSMAN.

"Sheriff's across the street. Want me to drop your bag at Kate's?"

"I'll take it with me."

With a grunt, Leider freed himself from the steering

11

wheel; stood up, walked around, and opened the trunk. "I won't go in with you. Plenty of work to do. But say hello to Kate for me. And tell her to call when she gets out. About the tasting. She'll know which one."

They shook hands. Leider's was puffy and soft.

Spraggue crossed the dusty street and walked up the concrete path.

He hadn't expected the high-rise modern office building. On one of the tall glass doors a hand-lettered sign read JAIL. The bold arrow underneath pointed off to the left. Spraggue hesitated for a moment, then chose the center door.

Chill, refrigerated air hit him in the face. The whole first floor of the place seemed, at first glance, to be a reception area. A counter topped with a slab of orange formica kept outsiders at bay. "Restricted" signs decorated the doors behind the counter.

"Yes?"

"Sheriff. . ." What the hell had Leider said his name was? "Sheriff Hughes, please." That was it.

"The sheriff's not in at the moment. What is it in regard to?"

They must have taught her that phrase when they hired her, Spraggue thought. "I'm here at the request of Kate Holloway."

"Holloway." The woman tucked the tip of her tongue firmly between her teeth, ran her finger down a list affixed to a clipboard. "Deputy Enright is handling that investigation."

"Then I'd like to see Deputy Enright."

"I believe he's using the sheriff's office. Why don't you go in there—that door marked ADMINISTRATION—and see if his secretary can help you?"

"Thanks."

A glass window peered in at the sheriff's outer office. That, too, had an orange counter blocking access. The decor was Holiday Inn: gold carpet, spindly turquoise chairs. Wall-to-wall vulgarity.

Spraggue pushed open the door.

The room had its own atmosphere, a bluish haze of cigar, cigarette, and pipe smoke. The lone secretary's desk boasted two huge ashtrays, one jammed with butts, the other issuing smoke signals from a lipstick-stained filter tip.

Spraggue gave his name to the sweet-faced graying woman behind the desk and asked for information about Kate. She nodded, puffed her cigarette, and pointed vaguely to a chair. He set down his carry-on bag and moved a chair upwind of the desk, to a vantage point where he could almost see around the corner of the L-shaped office. The secretary frowned at his rearrangement, but refrained from speaking.

"Are you going to tell someone I'm here, or do you use telepathy?" he asked mildly after a five-minute silence. He'd finished checking out a two-by-four board on which someone had mounted every imaginable kind of illegal drug paraphernalia. A larger board decorated with illegal weapons, from sawed-off shotguns to wicked-looking spiked chains, kept it company.

"I pushed the bell," the secretary said firmly. "Did you know that all those weapons were confiscated right in this county?"

"Push it again," Spraggue said. "Use the code for hostile people in a hurry."

She puffed furiously at her cigarette. "Are you the Holloway woman's lawyer?"

"No."

"Oh." There must have been a special code for lawyers. She shook her head sadly. "I've informed the deputy in charge. I'm sure he'll be glad to see you as soon as he's available."

"Give me a hint," Spraggue said. "Is he eating lunch? Manicuring his toenails? Is somebody else in there with him?"

She retreated behind a wall of smoke, leaving Spraggue to work on a new approach. Sometimes making yourself unpleasant in waiting rooms got you into main offices faster—the get-rid-of-the-nuisance response. Sometimes the offended secretary kept you cooling your heels even longer—the get-even response. Sometimes the only effect was an inner one: you felt better. Or you felt like a fool.

Spraggue got up, marched to the window, opened it.

"The windows in these offices are to remain closed. Open windows interfere with the air-conditioning system."

"Cigarettes interfere with breathing. Would you care for an earful of insights from an intriguing Japanese study on the harmful effects of nicotine, tar, carbon monoxide—"

She stalked away from her desk, disappeared around the bend in the L. Spraggue strained to hear distant whispers.

He leaned out the window, took a deep breath. No California health freaks in this office. No bean-sprout sandwiches in the sheriff's domain.

It was lucky there was no doorway between the sheriff's office and his secretary's. The man who entered the room would have taken the sides of the door down with his shoulders. Maybe the transom, too, with one blow from his shiny-domed forehead. Probably never notice the destruction in his wake either. Whereas Phil Leider was fat, this man was just *big*. He was the source of the cigar smell. Didn't have one on him now, but the stink came into the room like a cloud around his massive body.

"Name?" he asked, towering over Spraggue. His voice was tenor, rather than the bass it should have been. From his tone, Spraggue expected a speeding ticket.

"Michael Spraggue."

"Your interest here?"

"Prisoner Holloway, sir." Spraggue stopped short of saluting. He clicked his heels together silently. The secretary noticed.

"Miss Kate Holloway? Just what would that interest be? Boyfriend?"

"Business."

"Oh."

Spraggue waited.

"Do you have a business connection with a Mr. Leonard Brent?"

"He's an employee."

"Ah." The big man stared down at him, and Spraggue felt as if he'd been filed and cross-indexed. "Then you knew him personally?"

"Yes."

"Would you mind trying to identify him?"

"I came to see Kate Holloway. Is she here?"

"You'll see her a lot faster if you cooperate."

"If Holloway couldn't identify your corpse, I don't see how I could. She knew him better."

"I don't doubt that. It's just that the little lady turned squeamish on us."

The little lady. Spraggue bit the inside of his cheek. If anybody tried that one on Kate, he'd *better* do his talking through iron bars.

"If I check out your corpse, I get to speak with her," Spraggue said.

"For a few minutes. I think I can arrange it."

"Has she been charged?"

"Just a material witness. So far."

"I wouldn't mind taking a look at your corpse."

"Fine. Got a car outside?"

"No."

"I'll drive then."

"All right if I leave my bag here?"

"Nobody'll steal it."

The huge man led Spraggue into the sheriff's office and out through a back door barely big enough for him. They wound through a corridor to an exit and a squad car.

"Morgue far from here?"

"No morgue. Not many murders. Couple car crashes every year right after high school lets out. That's about it. We've got arrangements with local funeral parlors. This corpse is up at Morrison's. Right next door to the police station in St. Helena."

15

"And why isn't Kate at the police station in St. Helena? Why the county sheriff's office?"

"Body was found on unincorporated land. That's county."

They took First Street back to Route 29, traveling well within the speed limit. The deputy made a point of slowing down at each small town they passed through: Oak Knoll, Yountville, Oakville, Rutherford. On the outskirts of St. Helena he broke the silence with a statement that turned up at the end like a question.

"So you're Kate Holloway's partner?"

Spraggue didn't think it needed an answer. Instead he said, "And you are?"

"Captain Enright. Head of the detective bureau." He paused a moment, then continued with satisfaction in his voice. "So you're the one the little lady calls to come and get her out of trouble."

"Holloway called to tell me she'd have a hard time taking care of the crush from the inside of a cell. I'm here to hire a temporary winemaker. Until Lenny turns up."

"If Lenny turns up."

"Yeah."

"You call her 'Holloway'?"

"She calls me Spraggue."

"Seems disrespectful somehow. 'Course, 'Miss' is a funny thing to call her too. Couldn't rightly say she's a maiden lady."

"I'd be very careful what I called her, if I were you," Spraggue said.

Abruptly, the captain pulled the car over to the curb, right in front of a fire plug. "Out," he said gruffly.

The sign in front of the Spanish-style white stucco said MORRISON FUNERAL CHAPEL. The roof was red tile.

Enright banged on the side door.

It flew open immediately, revealing a smiling blond man with a ruddy face. Only the deep creases at the corners of his eyes kept him from looking like some gawky out-of-place teenager. And the badge on his tan shirt.

"Hi, Captain," he drawled cheerfully, a trace of the

South in his deep voice. "Got somebody else to take a peek?"

Enright shouldered the younger office aside and they entered a small waiting room. Spraggue counted to one hundred, tried to relax; his stomach was gearing up for the ordeal.

"Stay here," said the young man. "Only be a minute. I'll get the body ready for viewing. Got to keep it refrigerated—"

"Quit gabbing," said Enright.

"Right."

Spraggue watched the second hand on a wall clock go around twice. This was no waiting room for families and friends of the deceased. No statues, no flowers, no strait-laced formal furnishings. Just a delivery room: corpses in, corpses out.

"Okay." The reassuring voice of the red-faced officer came from the doorway. "Just walk on in. Nothing to alarm you. All covered with a sheet."

Enright snorted. "What do you think this is? A garden-club display?" He bowed slightly to accent the scorn in his voice. "Do come in, Mr. Spraggue."

They entered the dingy back room in close formation. It had a brick-red floor with a central drain. A refrigeration unit in a corner hummed loudly. A faucet dripped. Strong hanging lights illuminated a central slablike table covered with a still white sheet. Enright ripped it back.

"Think that's your Lenny Brent?" he said.

Only Enright's nastiness and the fact that he'd snubbed the airline's attempt at lunch saved Spraggue from following Kate's example and vomiting on the floor. He took a deep quick mouth-breath so he wouldn't smell the combination of decay and embalming fluid and played the scene like an acting exercise. An observation exercise.

The man on the table had a body but almost no head. A tall body, like Lenny's. A thin-to-medium body marred by a huge butterfly incision. The autopsy wound had been closed with gigantic uneven stitches. There was dark hair on the legs and torso, under the arms, at the groin. A white cardboard tag dangled from a big toe. The skin seemed terribly white. Spraggue forced himself not to look away.

The head. He'd probably had dark hair. A slightly prominent jaw.

"That your boy?" repeated Enright. The captain's voice was hoarse.

"No."

"No? Just 'no'?"

"You had a medical examiner look at this?"

"Forensic pathologist. Couldn't tell us much. Yet."

Spraggue nodded. "Lenny was about forty. Older than this guy. But he was in top physical shape. Exercised. Lifted weights. Look at this guy's arms. He sat at a desk."

"Of course, you wouldn't want it to be Lenny..." began Enright.

"What I want doesn't change a man's shape. Find somebody else who knew Lenny, somebody who worked out with him."

"*Miss* Holloway couldn't seem to—"

"Enright, she got sick," protested the young man. "The way you brought her in here, with no warning or anything—"

"Shut it, Bradley. Just shut the mouth."

"Okay. No beef."

Enright went on as if the interruption hadn't happened. "Mr. Spraggue, you say this is definitely not the body of Leonard Brent. Do you know whose body it is?"

"No."

"Go ahead and look more carefully. Plenty of time."

Spraggue kept his voice nonchalant. "No need. I don't know who it is. I *do* know that someone made a mistake and kept Kate Holloway in custody overnight for the murder of an unknown person. Her lawyer will be interested."

Enright grunted.

"Has the cause of death been determined?"

The captain guffawed. "Cause of death?" He nodded at Bradley to make sure he got the joke. "Practically missing his head, this fellow is. I figure that might have something to do with it."

"The head injuries could have been caused after death. Was there much bleeding?"

"I don't think," Enright said flatly, "we have anyone crazy enough around here to go beating up on a dead man like that."

"How about somebody smart enough to want you to have a hard time identifying the body? Got anybody that smart?" If they did, Spraggue was pretty sure he or she wasn't working for the sheriff.

Enright said nothing.

"I suppose you've taken prints?"

"Amateurs are always crazy for fingerprints. Not everybody's prints are on file, you know. Just if you've been in the army or gotten yourself arrested or something. Hardly anything gets solved by prints. Bet yours aren't on file anyplace."

"Wrong."

"Yeah?"

"Check with the Boston Police."

"Didn't take you for a crook."

"Guess again."

"Why've they got your prints?"

"Standard procedure when you get your private investigator's license."

Enright's lips tightened. "Let's see it."

Spraggue hunted through his wallet for a silent minute. "Here."

The captain grabbed the plastic-covered rectangle, held it closer to the light. He stared down at the tiny photo, then up at Spraggue.

"This is nothing but a piece of shit," he said. "Six-one, one-seventy, brown hair, brown eyes. The damned picture's so small it could be anyone. Your eyes don't look brown. And to top it all off, the thing's expired!"

"I know."

Enright turned on his heel. "Crap," he said loudly. "Bradley, when you get this mess cleared up, take Mr.

P. I. Spraggue over to the jail to see Miss Holloway. I got things to do."

His boot heels broke the silence.

"You can wait outside," Bradley said after the door had slammed. "Get the smell out of your nose." He covered the battered thing on the table with the sheet.

"Thanks." Spraggue moved toward the door.

"Don't mind Enright so much. He's got a bad stomach. Always acts up in here."

"That why he gave Kate Holloway such grief?" Spraggue asked sharply.

"Misery loves company, so they say. He'd have gotten along with you a lot better if you'd turned green and thrown up. Now he's got to prove he's tougher than you."

"He must be a pleasure to work with, Officer Bradley."

"Lieutenant Bradley. Brad." The ruddy face got even redder.

"Okay, Brad, why did you keep Kate Holloway in custody?"

"Body was found at Holloway Hills." The answer came out almost on time.

"It's a big place," Spraggue said. "No fences. Anyone could get in."

Bradley hesitated. "I suppose when they thought it was this guy Lenny..."

"Yeah?"

"Well," Bradley said weakly, "the valley's like a small town, really. You hear a lot of gossip."

"Such as?"

"I repeat gossip to you and Enright'll have my head looking like this dude's. Sorry. Go breathe outside for a spell. I'll be right along."

Outside, he inhaled audibly, deeply. Filled his lungs with sweet fresh-mown grass, stale car exhaust, and the first faint stink of deceit.

3

Lieutenant Bradley wound up doing double duty as chauffeur.

When he and Spraggue drove past the sheriff's office twenty minutes later, Kate Holloway sat slouched on one of the stone benches out front, Spraggue's duffel bag at her feet.

Bradley braked to a halt. "I'll be damned," he said. "So that's why Enright walked out on you. Figured you'd be so pleased to see her, you might forget to holler about violated rights."

"Not so dumb after all," Spraggue said, swinging the car door open. "Thanks."

"Wait up. She hasn't got a car here, and neither do you. Cabs are plenty scarce."

"We'll manage."

"Well, I'll malinger around back fifteen minutes or so just in case. Be glad to drop you someplace."

"Fifteen minutes." Spraggue banged the door shut and strode quickly up the concrete path. He knew that if he stopped to think of what to say to her, he'd turn to stone before the right words came.

Kate huddled sidesaddle on the bench, legs drawn tight against her chest, arms wrapped around them—folded into the smallest possible space. Her pointed chin rested against denim-covered knees. His footsteps startled her. She turned abruptly and began to rise.

"Don't bother." He peered down at her pale face and hesitantly touched her cheek. "You okay?"

"Sure. Don't overdo the concern."

"You look good."

"Is that supposed to make me feel better? You think I care how I look just now?"

"I'm trying to say I'm happy to see you, Kate."

"Okay." Her fingers plucked at his sleeve. "Then I'll try to say thanks for getting me out of that hellhole."

"Want to talk?"

"Not here." She shuddered. "Not this close . . . Captain Baboon might dream up another reason to put me away."

"There's a much nicer officer idling his engine around the corner. He'll take us home if you want."

She didn't answer.

"Come on," Spraggue said. She shook off his hand when he tried to help her up.

Kate standing had nothing defenseless about her. An inch over six feet tall, she looked Spraggue straight in the eye. She seemed smaller because she was thin, model thin, with dark, sleek, waist-length hair and Indian cheekbones. Men pestered Kate on the streets of L.A. with movie offers. She invariably refused, and when the would-be producers heard her speak, the legitimate few were relieved. She had a deep, foghorn voice, almost like a boy's, permanently arrested in mid-puberty.

Bradley was waiting, good as his word, sipping coffee from a red plastic thermos. After initial greetings, the ride was silent, the atmosphere strained. Bradley sped up the Silverado Trail, didn't have to ask directions until they passed Taplin Road. He dropped them at the gate: Kate's instructions.

"I've been cooped up way too long," she said after Bradley had driven off. She stretched out her arms and rolled up the sleeves of her plaid shirt. "Let's stay outside for a while."

Spraggue sounded out his stomach, found the funeral home experience over. "Lunch?" he suggested. "I'll buy."

"Business expense?"

"What else?"

She opened her mouth to reply, but then backed off, decided not to read anything into his response.

"Look," she said instead, "there's bread and cheese in the house. You can fetch it when you dump your bag. And a bottle of wine. We'll picnic."

"Where?"

"You know."

Spraggue got lunch together. They climbed up to the clearing, Kate hugging the bread and cheese, Spraggue toting the wine. Their target was halfway up the hill, a circle of soft grass and clover bounded by bushes, three large flat rocks, and yew trees. One of the few places in the valley with no view of vineyards, it stared straight up into the mountains. Starlit nights, years ago, they had . . .

Spraggue shook his head, eyed Kate warily. Had she brought him up here to reminisce, or did she still use the clearing . . . as a meditation corner, a rendezvous to meet new lovers?

"The bushes are overgrown," he said. "Trees are taller."

"Because you've been away too long."

"Looks the same to you?"

"I come up here pretty often, Michael. For lots of reasons. I didn't think you'd mind."

"Sit on the rocks?" he said. The bread and cheese were fresh, the wine heady. They ate without any polite small talk, greedily.

"Had enough?" Kate said finally.

"Too much. Cameras put pounds on you. I have to be gaunt by Sunday."

"More wine?"

"Enough for an afternoon."

23

Her hand reached for his, held on. "Do you want to get reacquainted?" she said softly.

"Reacquainted?"

"Do you want to revive old memories, Spraggue? Make love? Or have sex?" Her lips bore the ghost of a smile, but her dark eyes were unreadable. Her fingers toyed with the top button on her shirt.

Spraggue shoved their wineglasses into the comparative safety of a cleft between two rocks. He reached out and tilted her turned-away chin toward him. Her face was impassive. "Katharine," he said gently, but he knew he used her full name only in anger, "why the hell do you find it easier to sleep with men than talk to them?"

He knew as soon as he said it that he should have said "me" rather than "men," because she took it as an attack against what he'd once called her "unfaithful ways," not as a plea for more than physical communication. Shit, maybe he'd meant it as an attack, following the old pattern. If her way to avoid talk was sex, his was battle.

"Why the hell do you try to goad me into slapping your face?" she said.

"Sorry."

She didn't seem to notice the muttered apology. "What do you want from me, Spraggue?" she went on. "How do you know what I do with other men? Maybe I'm a vibrant conversationalist with other guys. Maybe we never go further than holding hands. Maybe you're the only one I don't know how to talk to."

"Don't you think we should try?" he said. "Considering the circumstances?"

Instead of answering, she made a production out of cleaning up the two cloth napkins, shaking the crumbs out to leave for the birds, folding them neatly and using the wine bottle to weigh them down against a gentle breeze.

"Dammit, Michael," she said finally, "I thought it would be easier. I've been in jail on suspicion of murder. Idiots yelled questions at me most of the night. The mattress they gave me wasn't more than a quarter-inch thick, and it felt like crumbled cardboard and smelled like ammonia.

24

I'm exhausted and I don't think I can go through what we always go through when we're together . . . and we're not really together."

"Wonderful," Spraggue said shortly. "So you decided to offer yourself as some kind of sacrificial lamb. You can get me out of the way and we can go on to other, more important things."

"Maybe it's not so important to me who I screw anymore. You don't like that, do you? Coming from me?"

"You're just trying to get me to slap your face and then we'll be back on familiar ground. Right?"

"God," Kate said wearily, "why can't we behave the way civilized people are supposed to?"

"Want to try? You can shake the napkins out again and I can sweep the grass. You pick up the stray leaves. I'll change the water in the squirrel's dish."

She shot him a feeble smile.

"How are you, Kate?" he asked. "Really."

"Eh." She shrugged her shoulders and shook back her long dark hair. "I'm okay. I like it out here. I'm going to be a damn good winemaker someday. You?"

"Not bad."

"The movie?"

"It's not going to set the cinema world on fire. Probably won't even be released."

"Are you married? Or engaged? If you are, I withdraw my offer."

"Neither."

"Why?"

"I haven't found anybody who's just like you—except different."

She smiled. "How different?"

"Less demanding. Somebody I could live with."

"You couldn't stand the lack of challenge."

"I'm thirty-four," Spraggue protested. "I'm getting tired of fighting."

"I'm the one who spent the night in jail."

"And what's that all about Kate?"

"I don't know." She stood up, and for a minute Spraggue

25

thought she was going to walk away, but she just circled the clearing once, then settled back down in the grass near his feet, facing away from him, gazing up at the blue-shrouded hills. He leaned forward and spread his hands on her shoulders, started to massage the base of her neck. She tensed at the first contact, but didn't pull away.

"When did you last see Lenny?" he asked.

She counted on her fingers. "Three days, four days . . . Sunday night."

"Doing what?"

"He wasn't dying, Spraggue, if that's what you mean."

He pressed down firmly on her shoulder blades. "Relax. Did he say anything about taking a trip, about anyone he wanted to see?"

"No. Not that I remember."

"Is your memory failing?"

"No," Kate snapped.

"Then you weren't paying attention to what Lenny said."

"Maybe not."

He moved his thumbs in a circular pattern down her spinal column. She sighed and flexed her shoulders.

"Where were you?" he asked.

"In the house. The kitchen, to be exact."

"Eating?"

"We had coffee."

"And there was nothing unusual about your conversation? As far as you could tell, Lenny planned to be out in the vineyards first thing Monday morning."

Spraggue kept rubbing her back, feeling the taut muscles under the thin shirt. He wished he could see her face.

"Yes?" he prompted.

"We had a fight, Spraggue."

"Ah."

"Yeah."

"Great," he said. "You went a few rounds with Lenny right before he mysteriously disappeared. A real screamer, I suppose."

26

She turned and looked up at him. The corners of her eyes crinkled. "Do I scream?"

"A real screamer," Spraggue repeated.

"Ouch! Not so hard."

"Sorry. Loud enough for any passing patrol car or nosy cellar-crew kid to get an earful. Lenny gets mad, takes off. You call the cops. They find a body. You're candidate number one."

"I didn't plan it that way," Kate said. "More to the right."

"Here?"

"Mmmmmmm."

"What did you fight about?"

She turned again. This time her eyes were hard black diamonds. "Technology, Spraggue," she said, overpronouncing each syllable. "We fought about the harvest. I wanted to take a sugar level twice a day for the next week, and Lenny—you know him and his damned 'artistry'— he didn't want me to. Didn't want any 'chemistry' involved. Wanted to go on the look and the feel and the taste of the grape. Why did I hire him if I wanted a chemist? You know. I got the whole Lenny-European-wine-grower-crush-the-grapes-with-his-own-feet routine."

"You knew he'd pull that when you hired him."

"I knew it, but I didn't really *believe* it. I didn't agree not to fight with him about it! There's got to be a balance between art and craft somewhere! Lenny was impossible."

"Was?"

"*Was* then, *is* now, I assume. I doubt he's suddenly gotten religion and become a humble monk at Christian Brothers." She pulled away, turned, and lay back on the grass. Spraggue thought she was even more beautiful at thirty-two than she'd been at nineteen. The shadows under her eyes gave her a bruised, vulnerable look. The longing to hold her, to accept her offer of easy, uncomplicated coupling came over him so suddenly he had to glance away. The moment wouldn't happen again. If they

27

slept together, if they even stayed in the same house, it would be on uncertain terms now, delicate ground.

"Could you stick around, Spragque?" she asked, shading her eyes with her palm. "Until Lenny gets back? I'm not sure I can handle the crush alone."

"You're just tired."

"No. Really."

"You could get Howard to come in."

"Ruberman? You think he'd fill in for Lenny?"

"Maybe."

"Not if I asked him. He took it hard when I let him go."

"I could ask."

"Go ahead. But I'd rather have you."

Spragque smiled. "I've done my stuff. You're out of the clink, and I've got location shots to film in Boston."

"You said the movie didn't start until Sunday."

"Your memory's coming back."

Kate rolled over on her stomach, pushing herself up into a kneeling position. She placed a hand on each of his thighs, peered into his eyes until he wondered what she could see. "Find Lenny," she said softly. "Stay long enough to find him. I really am worried."

"Where would I look? Who would I ask? I don't know my way around here anymore."

"I'll help. Lenny's got a place in Calistoga. No one answers the phone, but it would be just like him to be holed up there, sulking. I could ask Phil Leider—"

"He doesn't know anything. But he talked about it all the way up from San Francisco."

"So he did pick you up, the sweetie." A flicker of a grin crossed her face.

"Why the hell didn't you stop him? I might have wound up in some ditch."

"I thought you'd enjoy the experience. And he was only trying to help."

"He wasn't ticked off about Lenny?"

"You kidding? Don't waste your time worrying about Leider Vineyards. They're coining it. You should see the castle he just built. Swimming pool. Private screening room."

"How very Hollywood."

"Rumor has it he shows dirty skin flicks to a select few. I haven't been invited yet, but I have hopes."

"Where else should I look for Lenny?" He gave in with a grimace and a secret vow not to waste more than twenty-four hours at the task. "Girlfriend?"

Kate shrugged. "There's his ex, of course. I think she's somewhere back east. She may have heard from him. I don't know of any local contender."

"No gossip? You're slipping."

"If there is, you'll hear it soon enough."

Spraggue's right eyebrow shot up.

She laughed. "How do you do it?"

"The trick with the eyebrow? I'm not telling."

"No. How can you keep asking questions like that? Rattling them off like a cop?"

"Practice," he said. "I was once a private investigator."

"I will never understand that particular episode in your life, Spraggue. Want me to rub your back?"

He refused. The temptation was still there, clouding his judgment. She sat next to him on the rock, close but not touching. "I'm not sure I understand it," he said. "Romantic illusions, maybe. Mostly I dug up dirt everybody would have been better off not knowing."

She nibbled at the corner of a fingernail and shot him a sidelong glance. "So you went back to fantasy land. You and your actor eyes."

"Actor eyes?"

"They show exactly what you're thinking, what you're going to do next. They do, Michael. When you relax, they're like windows, but the minute you start asking questions, I can't see through them anymore. They glaze over."

"Otherwise I'd need a blindfold," he said. "Your eyes never give you away. I can't tell what you're thinking."

"Good," she said.

"Kate, I have to ask one more question."

29

"Shoot."

"Did you recognize that body?"

"Spraggue—"

"Come on. Someone put it where you'd find it. Or where you'd take the blame for it."

"I didn't find it. The cops did."

"Did they say why they looked? Why they just happened to check out the car trunk?"

"They didn't answer questions. They asked them. Like you."

Spraggue bent over and twisted a clover stem until it broke off in his hand. "Sorry."

"Spraggue?"

"Yeah."

"I really didn't recognize that body. But..."

"But?"

"But what if Lenny did?"

"He could have stuffed the body into that old car wreck, if that's what you mean. He certainly knew where the car was, knew that nobody was likely to disturb it."

Kate brushed a leaf out of her hair, wound a strand tightly around her index finger. "Then that could be why he disappeared...."

"The timing would be about right."

Kate stayed silent, closed her eyes.

"Do you still want me to find him?" Spraggue asked.

"Yes."

4

KATE WAVED HIM OUT OF SIGHT, LEANING BACK AGAINST
the railing of the sagging white porch. Déjà vu. Spraggue
sucked in his breath. Seven years ago . . . Hell, seven years
ago was seven years ago. Now was now. They'd have to
rip the old house down soon and build something showier,
nostalgia or not. With a tasting room for the tourists.
Holloway Hills wasn't amateur stuff anymore. Not with
over ten thousand cases projected for the '80 harvest.

Lenny's place was barely more than a shack, isolated
on a mountain road just beyond the Calistoga city limits.
Spraggue drove by once, no more slowly than the winding
road demanded. No car in the narrow gravel driveway.
A total absence of light in the grimy front window. He
made a careful three-point turn, parked Kate's gray Volvo
behind a dense stand of thorny bushes, out of sight of the
road. If Lenny suddenly opted for the quiet of home, he'd
never spot it. Nor would it give any passing squad car
pause. Soon enough the police would quit thinking about
Lenny as the victim. Then they'd consider him as the

suspect. One man dead; one man missing. In Boston it might take months to tie the two together; in Napa, hours.

Kate had left a worn pair of grease-stained work gloves lying on the dash—some things never changed. She had big, mannish hands, bit her nails to the quick, never wore rings. Still, the gloves were tight. Coarse-woven cotton, they'd stretch.

He knocked at the front door. No answer. Knocked at the back, admired the door locks, peered in a dirty curtainless window. Didn't look as if Lenny had much worth protecting with two new Yale deadbolts. No windows left ajar, not even the smallest. And no picklocks in his pocket. Damn.

Enright seemed like the type who'd personally twist the thumbscrews for breaking and entering. Out-of-town private investigators were pretty unpopular even if they kept to the letter. And he wasn't even a licensed P.I. anymore, just a nosy actor.

Before a defeated return to the car, almost as an afterthought, he lifted a corner of Lenny's soggy welcome mat. A single brass key glittered in the mud.

It turned easily in the front-door lock.

Hard to imagine Lenny, perfectly groomed, arrogant Lenny, living in such filth. The stench came mainly from the kitchen, a different stink, thank God, than the sweetish smell of death that hung over the funeral home. A smell, nonetheless, that Spraggue had little desire to investigate. He peered into the empty kitchen, noted the moldy dishes in the sink, and retreated, closing the door behind him.

The living room was covered with dust. When he walked, he kicked up a cloud in his wake. Certainly, Lenny hadn't lived here, not for the past six months or more. Unless he truly had a mind above housecleaning.

Some men did. Divorced men, especially. Got used to being cared for by a woman, then refused to accept that the former wife had actually performed services that could be missed, refused to accept the responsibilities of living alone. Men like that generally married again soon. And again. And again.

Sprague opened a door and entered a different world.

It must have been an enclosed back porch once, added on after the rest of the house was completed. If Lenny had used the back door, kept the door to the rest of the house shut, eaten only in restaurants, he'd never have seen the filthy half of the place. No need. The large pine-paneled back room had a bath off to the right. The gold tile in the bathroom almost matched the shaggy carpet on the bedroom floor. A closet door stood ajar, revealing a generous interior. Lenny's children, infants so young their sex was indeterminate, smiled out of framed photos displayed on an untidy rolltop desk. Sprague stopped short of opening the heavy gold-and-red print draperies, pressed the button on the base of a brass bedside table lamp instead. The air, stale with lack of circulation, carried no unpleasant smells. The linen on the double bed was fresh.

He inspected the closet. Row after row of neatly pressed shirts, laundry tags still affixed to collars. Suits in plastic cleaner bags. A pile of luggage on the floor to one side. No gaps where a suitcase had been hastily removed, an armful of shirts quickly packed inside.

The three-drawer bureau by the side of the bed was well organized. No missing piles of folded underwear.

Only in the bathroom was there any sign of planned departure. The mirrored cabinet over the sink was empty. No toiletries, no cold remedies, no toothbrush.

Where do you go with only the clothes on your back? Just your toothbrush? Just your shaving gear?

Sprague rummaged through Lenny's desk, taking care not to disturb the piles of receipted bills. A few yellowed letters. No plane schedules. No diary. No appointment book. After a moment's hesitation, he pocketed a thin black address book.

The four shelves over the desk held an array of camera equipment. No help there.

He sat on the bed while his eyes did a circuit of the room. The back door, the bathroom door, the door to the slum-half of the house. One unexplored door—probably cover for the cellarless dwelling's hot-water heater. He twisted the doorknob. Locked.

This one was easy. An American Express card did the trick.

Spraggue stared into blackness.

He groped around the inside of the doorframe, left and right. No light switch. He stepped inside, hands extended, touched a cold swinging chain, pulled it. Lenny's wine cellar leaped out of darkness.

Spraggue closed the door behind him. It was a good-sized cellar, maybe fifty cases in all, stored in the traditional cross-timbered bins. Spraggue lifted a bottle here and there and admired each label. Lenny had stored a selection of California's finest: rare old Georges de LaTours from Beaulieu, the first of Heitz's Martha's Vineyard vintages. More than enough justification for those fancy door locks.

Too warm, Spraggue realized suddenly. Despite insulation-padded walls and ceiling, the air was too hot for a wine cellar—seventy-five, maybe more. The air conditioner built into the far wall was silent. A blown fuse? Spraggue approached, found that the machine had been switched off.

Okay. He leaned against the wall and frowned in puzzled concentration. So Lenny kills a man, reason unknown. He rushes back to his house, takes only his toothbrush and aftershave, no clothes. Leaves in such a hurry he forgets to make sure the air conditioner is on. . . .

Not Lenny. Lenny would not have turned that air conditioner off. Even if he was halfway to Argentina by now, even if he had no plans ever to return and claim the wine, he'd have left the damn air conditioner going full-blast, and to hell with the electric bills.

Spraggue turned the machine on high. Tampering with evidence. He wasn't about to let that stuff turn to vinegar, any more than Lenny would have.

A different shape on a lower shelf caught his eye. A

large book with a thick leather binding, embossed and showy. Lenny's cellar book.

Christ, Lenny, Spraggue thought. Live in a pigsty, only clean the bedroom and bath. Come in the back door, never use your own living room. But keep a snobby leather binding on your tasting notes. He hoped no one would ever have to pry through his Cambridge apartment.

The air conditioner pumped away heroically, exchanging warm stale air for fresh cold. Spraggue crouched on the concrete floor and thumbed through the pages of the cellar book.

It was older than he'd thought, a winemaker's guide rather than a taster's memories. The first pages dealt with European wines, the wines Lenny had nurtured twenty years ago. His notes were complete and specific, giving grape tonnage, fermentation temperatures, cellar treatment. There was a small section for wines Lenny had drunk, not made. Here the comments were both cutting and colorful, including harsh personal remarks about more than one rival winemaker.

Spraggue flipped to the middle of the book: California, eight years ago. He and Kate had just bought the land for Holloway Hills.

He turned a page and found blank paper, loose blank paper, stuffed in to hide the fact that a third of the regular pages had been neatly sliced out. He read Lenny's final entry: August '74. It ended mid-sentence, mid-thought.

Had Lenny removed the pages? Spraggue searched for a second book, found none. Should he take the book back to Holloway Hills for further study? Couldn't slip this one easily into a pocket. Dust outlined its former place on the shelf. The sheriff's men might believe that Lenny had left his address book over at Kate's. His cellar book? Spraggue carefully replaced it on the shelf, turned off the light, closed the door. The steady hum of the air conditioner was audible from the bedroom.

No toothbrush. If Lenny lived here, Spraggue wondered, where the hell did he brush his teeth?

A black push-button phone on Lenny's bedside table

was still connected. Spraggue sat on the bed, pulled the address book out of his jacket pocket, turned to the *B*'s. The dial tone hummed in his ear. What was Lenny's ex-wife's name? There: Alicia . . . 428 Shore Drive, Marblehead. A 617 area code. Massachusetts.

Spraggue gave the operator his credit card number. Alicia Brent answered on the second ring, crisply, with her name.

"May I speak to Lenny?" Spraggue asked. His voice was deliberately lighter, younger, more hesitant and sibilant than usual. Alicia had only heard him speak once, maybe twice before.

The bang as she slammed the receiver back into the cradle made him jump. His right eyebrow shot up.

Alicia Brent. . . . They'd met at some wine-tasting publicity brouhaha, united by common disdain for the proceedings. A tiny woman, he remembered, so pregnant she was almost as big around as she was tall. Lenny Brent had ignored her completely, glad-handing his way through the throng. Spraggue had gotten the uneasy feeling that she was present by fiat, that she'd begged to be left at home. He remembered guiding her to a chair, planning a route to the nearest hospital, hoping a doctor had been invited to the brawl.

That had been eight years ago. And now, she hung up the phone when she heard Lenny's name.

He dialed the number again. It took eight rings before she made up her mind to answer.

Spraggue made his voice sound flustered, gentle, as unthreatening as his normally deep voice could be. "Uh . . . hello. I think we may have been cut off. I'm Roger Thurlow. You are Mrs. Alicia Brent, aren't you?"

"Yes," she said cautiously.

"I suppose you don't remember me. No. Well, I'm the National Secretary of Les Amis du Vin. We met at a tasting many years ago. . . ."

"You know that Lenny and I are divorced."

"Uh . . . yes . . . uh . . . I hope you won't think this an awful imposition. I, you see, I write the monthly asso-

36

ciation newsletter, and in this issue I'm supposed to print a biography of our October speaker. Mr. Brent, um, your former husband, is the speaker, but I can't seem to locate him to get the information I need, and I have to have the article in to the printer by tomorrow. Printing up a newsletter takes such a long time, and I'm really in a quandary. I know that he was born in Hungary and—"

"I am not about to—" she began angrily.

Shit, Spraggue thought. She was going to hang up again. He broke in quickly. "If you could just tell me some domestic details. You have children?"

Her voice was icy, but she stayed on the line. "Lenny has two lovely daughters he never sees. He's just as crummy a father as he was a husband. Is that the sort of thing you had in mind?"

"Well, uh, I don't think I could print that, Mrs. Brent. Our membership . . . I mean . . . there's a good deal of respect for Mr. Brent. He's a great man—"

"A great winemaker, maybe. *Not* a great man. Now I have to—"

"I really appreciate your talking to me. I was getting desperate. If you're ever in Napa—"

"I won't be."

"I thought you grew up out here."

"I did," she said woodenly, "but I won't be visiting."

"Well, one more thing then. If I needed to find your, uh, your ex-husband, for this biography thing, would you have any idea where I should look?"

The silence on the phone stretched out so long that Spraggue wondered if Alicia Brent were still there. He waited. If acting taught one thing, it was how to be comfortable with silence.

When Alicia's voice started up again, it seemed changed, cagey. "What did you say your name was?" she asked carefully.

"Uh . . . Roger Thurlow."

"Mr. Thurlow, I don't know where Lenny is. I don't care. Now I'm late for work. Please don't call again."

The phone clicked sharply. Spraggue jiggled the button

and a buzz came over the line. He kept the receiver pressed tight to his ear and replayed the conversation. Such vehemence about not visiting the valley, that sudden change of tone, the unmistakable suspicion toward the end.

He had to be back in Boston Sunday for the shooting anyway. Maybe he could wangle the time to call on Alicia Brent.

5

A YAWN TICKLED SPRAGGUE'S NOSTRILS. LENNY'S BED felt like a mixture of goose down and rose petals. Spraggue moved to a hard straight-backed chair.

Holloway Hills needed a winemaker fast. Kate would test the grapes, monitor the fermentation as best she could. She'd be in the lab now, checking the sugar content of each vineyard sample. But, as she always pointed out, she was still a technician, not a winemaker. Someday a winemaker, but for now, she needed Lenny. Or a Lenny substitute.

So coaxing Howard Ruberman back was top priority. He'd have to visit Howard next.

He appreciated Kate's reasons for not wanting to appeal to Howard personally. She and Howard didn't get along. No one got along with Howard. Not that he fought with people. Howard, Spraggue thought, rarely *saw* people. He treated them as if they were some species of mobile plant, nice enough to have around, but undeserving of words or smiles. Except when he fussed. Every day, something set him off, some piddling occurrence, trivial to anyone but Howard. For Howard, a grape falling on the floor was sufficient cause for a day of lamentation. What if this? What if that?

Kate had stated her reason for firing Howard simply: preserving her own sanity.

Spragye's eyes did a quick scan of Lenny's bedroom. Everything just as it had been, except that Lenny's address book was now in his jacket pocket. No extra fingerprints, thanks to Kate's gloves. But there would be footprints in the dust on the living room floor.

He found the broom in the cupboard of the foul-smelling kitchen, slipped the catch on the window over the sink just in case. Then he made his way to the front door, trailing the broom behind him to obliterate his prints. He left the broom leaning against the doorjamb. Captain Enright would realize that someone had been there. With luck, he wouldn't know who.

Luck held. Spragye stuck the key under the mat, returned to the car. He didn't pass another vehicle on his way back to Route 29.

Kate thought Howard had a room at the Calistoga Inn. "Incapable of taking care of himself" was how she'd put it. Spragye decided to stop by without phoning. Warning Howard would just give him more time to fuss.

Yes, they had a Howard Ruberman as a guest. The pointy-nosed man at the counter seemed surprised, as if requests for Howard were rare.

No, Mr. Spragye did not want to ring the room. He'd just knock.

The man shrugged as if he couldn't comprehend anyone walking up two whole flights of stairs when a simple phone call would suffice.

Howard was home. It took him a few minutes to answer the door, but Spragye could hear him bustling around inside, muttering "Just a minute" and "I'm coming." Footsteps finally clattered to the door, then stopped abruptly. "Who's there?" came Howard's querulous dried-up voice.

"Michael Spragye, Howard. Open the door."

"How do I know it's you?" The answer came after a

moment's hesitation and a little dance of anxiety tapped out on the floorboards.

"If you're so suspicious, you ought to have a peep-hole."

"They won't let me install one."

"Howard, have you got a chain? A chain lock on the door?"

"Yes."

"Well, use it! Open the door a crack and see if you recognize me."

More hesitation. "Stand back from the door."

"Okay."

"All the way across the hall."

"Howard, come on!"

The door inched open. Sprag... could barely spot the corner of a heavy dark pair of spectacles.

"Oh." The door closed, the chain jangled.

"That woman's not with you, is she?" Howard still sounded suspicious.

"I'm all alone."

"Good." The door opened. "Won't you come in?" Howard's scrawny body blocked the way. "Or maybe you'd rather we went down to the bar. They've rather a nice bar here. Not that I go there much, Mr. Sprag... "

"Michael," Sprag... corrected him, sidestepped, gained entry. "How are you, Howard?"

"Oh, not bad." Howard made an attempt at what must have been a laugh. "Not bad, Mr. uh ... Michael."

Howard's room, the room Kate had sworn he'd lived in since moving to the valley some ten years before, looked as if he'd moved in yesterday. A newspaper was neatly folded on the crisply made bed. Maybe that accounted for the time Howard had taken before opening the door. God forbid anyone should see him with his newspaper unfolded. Or maybe Howard had been reading something else. The cushion on an overstuffed armchair was slightly askew. Was that the corner of a magazine poking out from under it? Had Howard taken to the study of pornography

41

in his spare time? The thought both amused and saddened Spraggue.

Howard exuded nervousness. It came off him in waves, misted his heavy glasses, twisted his awkward hands.

"Instead of going to the bar, why don't we call down and have something sent up?" Spraggue said, taking charge. "We'll talk awhile and then I'll take you out to eat."

"That is kind. That's very kind. A good idea, too... only..."

"Only?"

"Let me call down to room service. What is the number? I always call it, but I never write it down, you know. White wine, I suppose. They have a nice Riesling. Château St. Jean. A little sweet, maybe, but before dinner ...well... Yes, I think I just dial nine. If I don't get room service, I'll get the desk and they can redirect me. Just a minute."

Spraggue waited while Howard relayed the distracted order, giving the wrong room number, correcting himself, and generally blabbing on for five minutes. Spraggue sighed. The longer he stayed in the room with Howard Ruberman, the more he understood why Kate had asked him to leave. And why he hadn't had a string of offers since Holloway Hills. Howard was no slouch as a wine-maker. As a person...

A hundred and twenty pounds—Spraggue wouldn't put Howard's weight at any more than that. Five-four, the weight ill-distributed along a tiny frame with narrow shoulders and a slight paunch. Howard looked even smaller than he was—as if his body were trying to shrink in on itself—stooping his shoulders and ducking his head. He wasn't old, Spraggue remembered. Maybe late thirties. He looked fifty. A bachelor hermit fumbling away at the phone, complicating a simple request into a conundrum.

Spraggue shook his head sadly. In spite of everything, he had a sneaking affection for Howard, some kind of sympathy for the colorless little man who'd gotten himself tangled in the phone wire. He'd once used Howard as the basis for a character in a play, slid right into Howard at the audition. He'd gotten the part.

Howard made it, a little breathless, over to the bed. He sat down.

"This is kind of you," he murmured, running his hands through colorless straw hair and realizing how long since it had been combed. "Kind of you, after what happened. I mean, the severing of our connections, our professional ties. Not that I blame Miss Holloway."

"For firing you?"

"It was that, that *Brent*." Howard spat out the name with more venom than Spraggue thought he had in him. "It was his fault."

"How?"

"Insinuating." Howard mulled over the word, nodded. "Yes. He *insinuated* himself with Miss Holloway. Oh, she was happy enough with Howard Ruberman before that. I mean, I'm not Lenny Brent, but I'm not a bad winemaker. I think Miss Holloway could still have learned a great many things from me, I really do. Technically, she has good instincts. Sound training, too. But Brent—"

The wine came, accompanied by a ludicrous routine of identity-proving, setting up a small table in the exact center of the room, tasting the wine, tipping the waiter. Spraggue was almost exhausted when the waiter finally backed out of the room. Howard could make any transaction complex.

When the commotion settled down and somehow Howard was back on the bed with a wineglass in his hand and, miraculously, the bottle safe and sound on the table and no shards of glass on the floor, Spraggue said quietly, "I didn't realize you knew Brent."

"Everyone knows everyone here. A winemaker knows another winemaker."

"How well do you know him?"

"Oh, not well, not well. I know his wine: Leider Vineyards, that is. He created some fine things, fine things. Big, moody wines. Complex. He has a way with Cabernet,

43

a gift. I thought he was happy at Leider's. I thought he'd stay put."

Sprague waited, sipped his wine. He had no right to ask Howard to continue his analysis of his successor. But if Howard was in a gabbing mood, he wasn't about to shut him down.

"Yes," Howard continued, after a pull on his wine-glass, "Kate Holloway, you know, she's such a good-looking woman." He blushed. "I noticed. Well, of course, she's a wonderful manager and a very smart woman, but she is good-looking, and, of course, I'm not very interesting to women. I never have been. And—"

"You think Kate hired Lenny because she wanted to get romantically involved with her winemaker?" Sprague tried to keep any inflection out of his voice.

Howard's hair seemed to stick out further in embarrassment. "No, no, that's not quite what I mean. Not Miss Holloway. Brent, he wanted my job. He *wanted* it. I mean, here in the valley, we compete, we complain, we exaggerate, we boast. But what Lenny did went beyond the limits. He wanted my job and he took it. I don't know what he said to Miss Holloway, or, er, what he did . . . But he took that job away from me. Miss Holloway wasn't dissatisfied with me. Oh, no. Not until that Brent, that damn Hungarian artist came visiting and probing and asking and hanging around and sneering at me and my wine! 'Technician,' he calls me. And 'chemist.' Not 'winemaker.' I'm not ashamed to be a chemist. I'm a very good technician!" Howard's voice, Sprague noted, got louder with each sip of wine.

"Was Brent unhappy at Leider's?"

"Must have been, mustn't he?" Howard giggled. "Maybe old Leider was going to fire him. Maybe he wouldn't give him a raise. Lenny Brent took care of his own interests, well in advance." Howard helped himself to a third glass of wine, slopping a little over the edge of the glass. "He took my job."

"Would you like it back?" The question hung in the air.

"What?"

"I'm asking if you want the job back."

"What about Brent?"

"He's missing," Spraggue said slowly. "Gone off somewhere, maybe. . . ."

"He'll rush back if he finds out you've hired me again," Howard said bitterly. "When he comes back, you'll give him my job. Again."

"I honestly don't think he'll be coming back."

"What if he does?"

"Unless he's back within the week, with a damn good explanation, an unassailable excuse, the job is yours."

Howard hesitated. "Coming back now . . . What? September? Late September. Full harvest already. I don't know that I'll be able to . . ."

Come on, Howard, Spraggue thought, come on! Hit me for a raise. Do something to get some self-respect back!

Howard babbled on. "Miss Holloway, she'll be taking care of things, so it won't be impossible. I'll have to get over there right away. I'll have coffee, lots of coffee. I won't be able to have dinner with you after all, then. No, just coffee, and I'll get to work."

"You can wait until tomorrow," Spraggue said.

"No, no. You won't be sorry you hired me. I'll work harder. The '77 Chardonnay is making a fine showing, you know, and I think this harvest will be a good one." He looked down at himself, rubbed his hands on his pants legs, ran them through his hair.

"I'll have to change clothes," he thought aloud. "I'll change and have coffee and get over there. Miss Holloway knows?"

"She asked me to speak to you."

"That was good of her. You'll see. I've hardly forgotten anything. In fact, I've learned, I've read. It hasn't been so long. Not long at all. A temporary aberration in the system, that's all. Now I do have to change. If you'll excuse . . ."

Spraggue stood while Howard dithered. On the way

out, curiosity moved him toward the armchair. He deliberately brushed against the crooked cushion. Howard's secret reading material was gone.

Howard offered a cold, shaky hand. "Good of you," he muttered. "You'll see ... won't be sorry ..." His voice trailed off and he turned away, leaving Spraggue to shut the door.

As he stood outside in the corridor, Spraggue heard the tiptoe approach of Howard's feet, followed by the twist, turn, and bang of shooting bolts and the jangle of the chain lock.

6

Spragge decided the ache in his gut was hunger, not a presentiment of disaster. He got the Volvo back on the road, pointed down Washington Street toward Route 29. Kate might have something edible at Holloway Hills—frozen or canned.

Thirty minutes from Calistoga to Holloway Hills, minimum. Estimated time before acute starvation: ten minutes. Better to eat along the way, he thought, in some quiet haven where he could rehearse the inevitable scene with Kate, the one they'd act out after he announced his morning departure for Boston. With Howard panting for his old job back, Kate wouldn't have any trouble with the harvest. And how much time could he waste tracking down Lenny Brent, especially if Lenny had the best of reasons to hide? The un-air-conditioned wine cellar gnawed uneasily at one corner of his mind.

Halfway through St. Helena, crawling along at a legal 25 mph, he thought of La Belle Helene. What he really remembered was soup, delicious cream of watercress, along with the faint image of a tiny restaurant tucked away

47

on a back street. He took a sudden left, then a right, trusting to instinct. Railroad tracks. He hadn't crossed railroad tracks the last time. He swung the Volvo in an unhurried U, backtracked, and smelled the restaurant before he saw the sign. A parking place beckoned right across the street.

The little museum next door was closed, its premises tacked on to the restaurant. Tables swathed in white napery shone in the window. Spraggue hesitated, opened the door.

It was easily three times the size he remembered—renovated and remodeled, too. The entryway now housed an antique banquette surrounded by potted palms. The crowd was dense, noisy. The wood-beamed ceiling—that was the same.

"Reservation?" inquired a dark-eyed man.

Shit, Spraggue thought and almost said.

"Michael Spraggue!" He didn't even have a chance to pivot and head for the door. His hand was seized and pumped by a blond, blue-eyed, aging California dreamboy.

"I thought it was you! The L.A. County Fair, the wine-tasting! On the tip of your tongue, isn't it? George Martinson! Wine and food reviewer for the *Examiner*."

So much for calm reflection, Spraggue thought.

Martinson kept a firm grip on Spraggue's elbow while his enthusiastic tenor bubbled on. "The wife and I dine here quite often. Join us. There's never an empty table on a Friday night."

Friday night? So it was. "I wouldn't want to in—" Spraggue started hurriedly.

"Nonsense, we'd love to have you. Right this way."

Spraggue found himself being dragged along through a maze of tables. "Michael Spraggue, owner of Holloway Hills," was the way Martinson introduced him to the plump, fortyish brunette at the table. She wore red, very low-cut, and must have saved one of her push-up bras as a souvenir of the fifties. Her name was Mary Ellen, she had a round good-natured face marred by a pouty mouth, and either she was hard of hearing or Martinson was anxious to broadcast the identity of his guest. Spraggue felt like a prize trout, well and truly hooked.

He sat down. A waiter rushed over and plunked a Plexiglas frame on the table, the menu handwritten on a card inside. Gone the days of the big central blackboard with choices scrawled, erased, scrawled again.

"You've already ordered?" Spraggue asked.

Martinson nodded. "White wine. There's more on the way." Spraggue raised an eyebrow; the Martinsons had already chalked up at least one bottle of St. Jean Fumé Blanc. The waiter placed the empty on his tray.

"Then I'll have the salmon. Soup to start." It was cream of lettuce, not watercress.

The waiter bustled off and the din of conversation closed around him.

Mary Ellen giggled and hid her heavily lipsticked mouth behind a ring-upholstered hand. "We actually ordered a bottle of *your* Chardonnay, the '77. And then I recognized you as soon as you walked in. I said to George, 'Isn't that Michael Spraggue? I wonder what he's up to here in the valley?'" Her mouth feigned innocence, but her eyes said that she knew exactly why he was here. Spraggue thought that Kate's brief imprisonment had probably served the Martinsons as appetizer. Damned if he'd be the main course.

He smiled. "I hope you like the wine. I'll be interested in your opinion."

"Interested?" Martinson laughed, showing off half a yard of glistening teeth. "Interested? My boy, you'll be *reading* my opinion. No punches pulled, either."

Spraggue's smile glazed over. Another joy he didn't feel up to right now was an in-depth wine rap. He loved drinking it, hated talking about it, and that was that. Holloway Hills was a damned successful investment, a product he liked that made money. It wasn't exactly the Home for Little Wanderers, but it wasn't like owning half of Consolidated Warheads either... and there'd been Kate....

"A little on the oaky side," Martinson led off. "I'm

with Louis Martini on that score: 'If you like oak, go chew a toothpick.'"

Mary Ellen giggled on cue. "Oh, George, he was talking about Zinfandel." She patted her dark hair and forced a smile. "What kind of oak do you use, Mr. Spraggue? Michael?"

Spraggue regretted joining them. A take-out burger and a plastic shake would have been preferable. "We age the Chardonnay in Limousin oak, the Cabernet in Nevers."

Mary Ellen grinned archly. "No American oak at all?"

Spraggue shrugged. "Holloway Hills goes for a classic French taste—"

Martinson ended his sentence, "—And Mr. Spraggue, dear Mary Ellen, wouldn't have to worry about the cost of those barrels. Three hundred, three hundred fifty dollars apiece these days."

"So they tell me," Spraggue said flatly.

"Howard Ruberman was your winemaker for the '77, wasn't he? That explains the oak." Martinson patted Mary Ellen's hand. "You know Howard and oak."

"Howard may be coming back to Holloway Hills." Spraggue dropped the bomb lightly. He could have sworn Mary Ellen's ears twitched.

"Then it's true!" she said, raising her voice in case any other diners were interested. "Lenny Brent is dead—and they've arrested—"

"All a misunderstanding, Mrs. Martinson." Spraggue's voice topped hers easily.

Her mouth closed and opened twice, like a goldfish feeding in a tank. "He's not dead," she said softly. "Oh." She drew in a sudden breath and Spraggue saw her husband's hand tighten abruptly over hers, pressing the rings into the soft flesh.

Martinson chimed in quickly. "Then you're tired of the great Brent already?" There was a sneer in his voice.

Mary Ellen giggled. She had quite a line in giggles; this one had no mirth in it. "George and Lenny didn't exactly see eye to eye...on wine." She caught her husband's glance, released her hand and quickly slipped it under the table. The red marks were plain.

"Everyone's entitled to his own opinion," Martinson said breezily, suddenly fascinated by one of the landscapes on the far wall.

"Well, Lenny wanted to offer far more than his opinion." Mary Ellen winked at Spraggue, an unmistakable wink.

"Really?" said Spraggue, following along, wondering if Brent had crossed swords with the entire valley. He thought back to his own meetings with the haughty vintner; it was possible.

Martinson's face turned slowly red. "Brent actually wrote to the managing editor of my paper, demanding that I print a retraction! A retraction of a tasting! What was I supposed to do? Alter my taste buds? Suddenly decide, two weeks after the fact, that I'd been wrong? What the hell does wrong or right have to do with tasting? I call them as I taste them, simple enough. But Brent couldn't see that. A conspiracy against him! God, the charges he made!" Martinson's voice lowered. "He hinted that I'd been paid off. Can you imagine? It got so I was afraid to answer my front door. The man's a menace. Personally, I think you're wise to be rid of him."

"I don't know that I'm rid of him exactly," Spraggue said.

Martinson raised his pale eyebrows.

"I just can't seem to locate him."

"During crush?" Martinson asked incredulously.

Mary Ellen looked as if she wanted to take notes, her mouth pressed into a thin line with a parenthesis on each end. "He *is* missing, then," she trumpeted happily. "And that's why the police—"

The waiter picked that moment to serve soup. The wine was brought and duly opened. The *Examiner*'s wine critic performed the appropriate ceremonies to the hilt.

"Well, I don't understand," Mary Ellen Martinson said bluntly, as soon as the waiter was out of earshot. "Wasn't there a body? I *heard* there was a body."

51

"Not Lenny's."

"Disappointed?" asked her husband under his breath. Mary Ellen stared at him coldly, turned her attention back to Spraggue.

"Do they know who died?" she asked.

"I don't." Spraggue sipped his wine. Howard was right; it was showing well. Fruity, but with acid to spare, and strong varietal character.

"Was it murder?"

"Seems likely."

They ate soup. Lines of concentration furrowed Mary Ellen's brow. She tried another giggle and changed the subject. "How long are you planning to stay in the valley, Michael?" She leaned way over the table. Spraggue kept his eyes on his soup.

"Till tomorrow morning," he said, "with luck."

"Then business is all settled?"

"Ruberman will be back as winemaker. He and Kate can handle the harvest without me."

"You're not tiring of the wine business?"

"No." Spraggue decided he'd answered enough questions. "Why do you ask?"

Another giggle. "Rumors. All these sell-outs to conglomerates."

"Nothing like that in the wind at Holloway Hills."

"If you say so," said Mary Ellen.

"Glad to hear it," said her husband.

The wine was starting to turn Mary Ellen's giggle into hiccups. "Don't suppose you know where Lenny's off to? Always was unreliable—not as unreliable as some—"

The clearing of soup plates and the advent of poached salmon with hollandaise sauce interrupted her. Then Martinson lead the discussion relentlessly into the topic of wine and insisted on ordering another bottle, a Chardonnay he swore bore some resemblance to Holloway Hills. Not until dessert did Spraggue manage to steer the conversation back to Lenny Brent.

"Were you and Lenny friends?" he asked Mary Ellen,

and was rewarded by seeing George gag on a mouthful of strawberry mousse.

Mary Ellen just giggled.

"Well, where would you look for Lenny if you wanted to find him?"

Martinson tried to answer first, but Mary Ellen jumped in before her husband could lower the napkin from his mouth.

"*Cherchez la et cetera,*" she murmured with a grin. "Always, in Lenny's case. I've *heard*," she added as an afterthought, directly to George.

"You know who the woman is?" Spraggue asked.

"It *is* a small valley." Mary Ellen was enjoying herself, stalling, adding cream to her already white coffee. "Just five miles wide and—"

Martinson interrupted. "There was that beautiful child, wasn't there? With the bizarre name? Remember?"

"*Very* well," Mary Ellen said. "*Grady*-something-or-other. A made-up name to go with the bottled hair color, absolutely the most incredible red you've ever seen!"

"A waif, you know," Martinson said, mouth gloomy, eyes sparkling. "Thin, with those big smudgy eyes, very Hollywood romantic."

"Thin?" Mary Ellen smiled broadly. "Last time I saw her she was far from thin. Expecting company, I'd say."

"Lenny's child?" Spraggue asked.

"A girl like Grady—she probably has no idea." Mary Ellen poured herself a very full glass from the new bottle of wine.

"And you think Lenny might be with her?" Spraggue tried to catch Mrs. Martinson's eye. Impossible.

"Do you like this wine?" She held her glass of golden liquid up toward the ceiling, peering at it through one half-closed eye.

Lavalier Cellars. Spraggue read the label, couldn't place the name. The wine seemed raw to him, unfinished, uncouth. No match for Holloway Hills. "Yes," he lied quickly. "Now—"

Mary Ellen swirled her glass, inhaled deeply. "You're going to be hearing about this wine. You bet your sweet—"

"I had the distinct feeling that this Grady was in Lenny's past," George Martinson said, "that he'd dropped her."

"Because of the child?"

"Who knows? According to the gossip—" Martinson stopped abruptly.

"According to the gossip," Spragque repeated painstakingly, "who would Lenny be with now?"

Mary Ellen giggled and sloshed her wine over the white tablecloth. "Rumor is that he's shacked up with Holloway Hills and Valleys—over at your place."

Martinson's shrug took in his drunken wife, the sodden tablecloth, the late hour, and Mary Ellen's revelation. "That's what I've heard, too," he agreed, almost apologetically. "Phil Leider told me he sure couldn't match Kate Holloway's offer!"

7

Spraggue didn't escape the Martinsons until La Belle Helene's staff practically threw them out at eleven-thirty. Their party was the last to quit the dining room. Spraggue felt the same relief he saw on the faces of the waiters.

Mary Ellen Martinson was falling-down drunk. George virtually carried her, his right arm viselike around her shoulders. His face had the slow flush of alcohol, but he bundled his wife off into the car in a businesslike fashion, as if he'd rehearsed the routine before. He pulled her red skirt down over her thighs.

"Ride?" he asked Spraggue.

"No, thanks. Sure you're okay to drive?"

Martinson's face reddened even more. "I have a great capacity for wine." He gazed discontentedly at Mary Ellen, slack-jawed and faintly snoring in the passenger seat. "Unfortunately, my wife does not share that gift."

The statement needed no confirmation. Spraggue banged Martinson's car door shut with more than necessary force and headed back to his car, glad he'd drunk so little of the wine, sorry that Mary Ellen had felt the need to compensate for his restraint.

What game were they playing, those two? A simple round of capture-an-innocent-bystander-for-dinner to alleviate their mutual boredom? Or a deeper charade? And what was Martinson up to, encouraging Mary Ellen to guzzle her drinks like a combat-zone pro, refilling her drained glass the moment she set it down, then lamenting over her limited capacity? The drunker she got, the wider her husband's grin. And now Martinson would chauffeur her home and stuff her into bed unconscious. How many nights a week did they play out that scenario?

A warning bell sounded somewhere in Spraggue's head, cautioning him to back off and leave such speculation strictly alone. Turn on some blaring radio station, it urged him. Memorize those movie lines. Anything to avoid getting snared in the spiderweb of strangers' lives.

How could he ever have been a private investigator? The answer may have puzzled Kate, but it was no mystery to Spraggue, just an outgrowth of the same desire to live other lives that drove him as an actor. How would you play a man like George Martinson? What made people tick and tick and keep on ticking years after the mechanism should have run down?

But acting wasn't life. Three years of delving into reality had taught him that there weren't any pretty painted proscenium arches to frame messy slice-of-life melodramas with meaning. No safe scripts with all the loose ends tied in careful knots. No resolutions, no illusions, no curtain calls. The best you could hope for was to shelter a tiny circle of loved ones from disaster. . . .

Kate was a throwback to a time before he'd learned that lesson, a time when he hadn't loved as cautiously.

The engine started smoothly. Spraggue drove carefully, keeping a tight rein. At least contemplating the Martinsons' bizarre relationship delayed thoughts of Kate. Kate and Lenny. . . .

"Stick around and help me, Spraggue. I'm not sure I can handle the crush all by my lonesome." Crummy dialogue, but better than "Stick around and help me find my lover." How would that line have gone over? Not half as well. Bad taste, begging the ex to find the present. And offering to sleep with the ex to seal the bargain. Shit.

He hadn't believed Howard, old unperceptive Howard. But Mary Ellen and George and Phil Leider. . . . How many witnesses did he need?

So Lenny and Kate had a winemaking spat Sunday night and Lenny ran off. Just like that. God, he wondered what the battle had really dealt with. Hadn't taken place in any kitchen over coffee, either. Not with Kate.

And that was the gossip Lieutenant Bradley wasn't authorized to clue him in on.

Spraggue jammed his foot down on the accelerator, too hard for the narrow twists of Zinfandel Lane. Lights blossomed in his rear-view mirror; he'd picked up an unexpected companion on the usually deserted road. He yanked his foot completely off the gas, let the car creep back to normal speed. Why hurry? He hoped Kate would be sleeping by the time he got back, knew she wouldn't be. Knew she'd be waiting, reading, in the old double brass bed, naked.

Shit. The anger blew out of him like air out of a punctured balloon. What right had he to pass judgment on Holloway's bedmates? He didn't own *her*, just half the winery. Didn't *want* to own . . .

The car was handling oddly. The next bump in the road left no doubt about that. When he hit the brake, it grabbed, swerving off to the right. He fought the steering wheel to keep the Volvo aimed down the center strip. That car behind him followed too closely.

Damn, Spraggue muttered under his breath. He groped for the emergency flashers, flicked them on, and swung over as far as possible toward the right-hand verge of the narrow road. The other car gunned its engine, whizzed past, roared out of sight. Spraggue stopped the Volvo dead, got out to check on a visible cause for the car's erratic behavior.

The night air was heavy with the smell of ripe grapes.

Vines stood thick all around, supported by wood and lashings of rope, bowed with the weight of the purple clusters. Spraggue stared straight up and took a calming, lung-filling breath. So many stars.

The right front tire was flat as Kansas. He'd never make it to Kate's, up that twisty driveway.

Not a car, not a house. That jerk behind him— Once, years ago, when a car displayed flashers, pulled off the road, the driver behind would stop, offer aid. Maybe Leider was right. Nobody did that anymore. Too dangerous. Better not to get involved.

Let there be a spare tire. Kate was notoriously negligent about such petty details. He retrieved the keys from the ignition. At least there were two on the chain. She could have just handed over the ignition key, never dreaming he'd need to open the trunk. Maybe she kept a flashlight in the glove compartment. Spraggue circled the car, opened the passenger door. Nothing in the glove compartment but used paper towels and a half-empty bottle of Windex.

Another car passed, didn't slow down even when he waved.

He left the right-hand door open for light. The glow barely reached around to the trunk. He fumbled with his hands for the lock before remembering the tiny pencil flash on his own key ring. He found it, clicked it on, tried the key in the lock. Rusty. He worked it for what seemed like minutes before the key turned and the trunk sprang open.

As soon as he smelled it, he was glad of the darkness, glad the stars were faint, faraway specks. Not masked by embalming fluid now, it was a sickly sweetish stink. He flicked off the pencil flash and turned away. He had no desire to see what was left of Lenny Brent. His knees wobbled and he straightened up with effort. The silence was so intense it seemed to hum.

The hum came closer. This time the passing car stopped. It had flashing blue lights and the sheriff's insignia over the door.

8

"WHEN CAN I SPEAK TO KATE HOLLOWAY?"

Shakespeare mirrored the fall of kings in foul weather. Lenny's death, Spraggue thought, glancing disgustedly around the sheriff's office in the early hours of Saturday morning, was rendered in stale smoke, filthy ashtrays, and the harsh glare of fluorescent bulbs.

Two hours since the discovery, two hours of hurry-and-wait, hurry-and-wait, punctuated by a single question, his own: "When can I speak to Kate Holloway?"

She was somewhere around the L-shaped bend, stashed in one of the tiny offices. That much, Lieutenant Bradley had leaked. Captain Enright wasn't communicating; he'd given it up with a satisfied smirk the moment Spraggue had identified the body.

Bradley barged out of the inner office. "Coffee?" he said, before Spraggue could gear up for the question.

"Thanks. Black." Spraggue stood and fumbled for change in his right-hand pocket.

"I'll take care of it. Seeing as you're an unwilling guest."

Spraggue wished Enright were the flunky they sent out

59

for coffee. He tried a variation of his request when Bradley returned with two steaming cups balanced precariously on a cardboard tray.

"Can I see Kate Holloway?"

"I doubt it. But hang around, by all means. Enright gets a charge out of knowing you're still here fuming."

"Is he talking to Kate?"

"Yeah. She stopped listening about an hour and a half back."

"I presume he knows it's illegal to question a suspect without a lawyer present."

"Oh, I suppose he made it clear that she doesn't have to say anything."

"Is he confining his agenda to Lenny's death?"

Bradley nodded, sipped coffee.

"Just a coincidence that two guys wound up stuffed in car trunks within the week?"

"I don't tell Enright how to run an investigation."

"Do you know how Lenny died?"

"No sign of violence. We're waiting for the autopsy report—"

"Which is confidential police business." Enright loomed around the L.

"When can I—" Spraggue began.

"You a lawyer?"

"No."

"Then get lost."

"A conviction was recently overturned by the Supreme Court because some cop in Iowa refused to let a suspect talk to his mother," Spraggue said.

"You her mother?"

"Let me try a more subtle approach: I will make one hell of a stink if I don't get to see Kate soon."

"Yeah?"

"And I hate to make trouble."

"I don't even think you *can*."

With effort, Spraggue willed his right hand to stay unclenched and harmless down at his side. If the deputy weren't so huge ... Hitting Enright would have the same

60

effect as pounding a frozen side of beef: broken knuckles. Worse. You didn't get tossed in jail for assaulting a dead cow.

"I'm starting to feel," he said, his smile not reaching his eyes, "the urge to make a handsome campaign contribution to anyone running against Sheriff Hughes."

Enright snorted. "Got to go to the can," he said. "Bradley, take over here for a while." His footsteps clicked down the hall. Spraggue wondered if he had king-sized taps stuck to his toes and heels to punctuate his swagger.

Bradley crumpled his empty coffee cup in his fist and dunked it into a corner wastebasket. "Come on. What he means is that I should get you and Miss Holloway together. Then he'll yell at me for knuckling under to you."

Spraggue followed Bradley around the L-shaped bend and through a warren of antiseptic hallways, finally turning into a small cubicle off a long corridor. In a chair sat Kate, pale as chiseled ivory, hands clasped tightly in her lap.

Bradley signaled to a severe woman in a tan uniform, who glided noiselessly away. He stationed himself just outside the door. "Can't really give you any privacy," he muttered apologetically. "No privileged communication or anything."

"How much time do we have?"

"How long does it take Enright to pee?"

"Can you call my lawyer?" Kate said, too calmly. "He might hang up on me—the lady who cried wolf and all that."

Spraggue leaned down and kissed her cheek. "We haven't got much time, so just answer me."

"In front of the jailer? Don't you think I killed Lenny?"

"Whisper. If you stashed him in the trunk, you wouldn't have loaned me the car."

"What do you want to know?" she asked softly.

"Were you sleeping with Brent?"

"Where did you get that tidbit?"

"Mary Ellen Martinson."

Kate glared at him for a moment. "When I said you'd

61

get the gossip soon enough," she said angrily, "I had no idea you'd head straight to the source."

"You weren't sleeping with him?"

"Does it matter? You think I'm more likely to murder a man I've had sex with?"

Their eyes locked, his challenging, hers defiant.

"Is that all?" she said.

"No. When I speak to your lawyer, I'm going to ask him not to bail you out."

"This better be good, Sprague."

"How's this? Act One: unidentified body found in abandoned car. Act Two: very identifiable body found in far-from-abandoned car. The play has only one continuing character: you. You played the chief suspect in Act One; you're doing an encore now. So maybe someone is killing people to put you in jail."

"You're kidding," she said, staring down at her jittery hands. "You're reciting dialogue from that detective movie of yours."

"Howard Ruberman isn't that fond of you. Mary Ellen Martinson—"

"If *she'd* been stuffed in the car, I'd need an alibi."

"She feel the same about you?"

"This is ridiculous."

"Keep your voice down." Sprague leaned back against the cool cement-block wall. "And tell me why people keep asking me if I'm planning to sell Holloway Hills."

"Mary Ellen say that?"

"Does it matter?"

"I got an offer on the place. I turned it down. That's all."

"Who?"

"United Circle. A good price. Should I have asked you?"

"You can veto any sell-out, Kate. Terms of the contract."

"I'd never sell."

"You told somebody from United Circle that?"

"Sure."

"Who?"

"Some guy . . . I don't remember . . ."

"They could think I'd be more willing to sell—"

"I said United Circle, Spraggue. Not the Mafia."

"What was the guy's name?"

". . . Baxter . . . just some stiff in a pin-striped suit."

Bradley had a sudden coughing fit. "Enright," he said out of the corner of his mouth before strolling tactfully toward the water cooler.

"Kate," Spraggue said quickly, "I'm sorry."

"For what?"

"Picking that fight on the hillside this afternoon, instead of—"

"Your loss," she said coldly.

"I know."

Enright's boot heels cleared the corner. "What in the devil is going on here?" He jerked his thumb in Spraggue's direction, glowered at Bradley. "Out!"

Spraggue smiled. "Her lawyer's on the way."

"Out."

"One thing. That squad car tonight, was that a regular patrol?"

Bradley answered. "Somebody called in and reported a vehicle in trouble. Gave your location."

"And before? How did you happen to look in the trunk of that abandoned car over at my place?"

Bradley stared at his shoes.

"Out," Enright repeated.

"Anonymous tip," Spraggue said flatly. "Right?"

Enright took a threatening step forward.

"Relax," Spraggue said. "I'm leaving."

9

SPRAGGUE INTENDED TO START OFF HIS INVESTIGATION
with a breaking-and-entering at Lenny's girlfriend's apartment.

Four scanty hours sleep hadn't exactly cleared the fog.
Twenty minutes in the shower, until the pounding water
turned too icy to bear, sharpened his senses and revived
his memory: Lenny's address book. And Mary Ellen's
snide advice: *cherchez la femme.*

Searching Kate's bedroom undid at least half the good
of the shower; he felt dirty again. An invisibly slimy in-
truder prying through bureau drawers, betraying trust with
prodding, curious fingertips.

Seven years had hardly changed her room. A fresh
coat of cream-colored paint, a different bedspread tossed
over the old cane-back rocker. The same black-and-white
framed studies of water lilies, dating from her amateur
photographer days. She still folded her underwear with
spartan neatness and scattered scarves and stockings over
the mirrored dresser top. Her scent clung to the scarves,
familiar and reproachful. When he lifted her pillow, a lacy

64

nightgown was stuffed underneath, just as he'd known it would be.

He examined the adjoining room, his old room, even more relentlessly. Kate never cared to spend the entire night with a man; connecting doors with a lock on her side, that was her preferred arrangement. He found no trace of Lenny; plenty of dust.

Five toothbrushes in the bathroom, some old, some new. Impossible to guess the gender of a toothbrush's owner.

Grady, then.

Spraggue rummaged through the kitchen cupboards until he found an unopened jar of strawberry jam. The English muffins in the cellophane packet on the countertop were stale. Toasted and drenched with jam, they'd pass for breakfast. He opened the refrigerator, surveyed Kate's meager supplies, made a mental list of survival groceries.

The toaster popped. The jam jar surrendered its top after he beat it repeatedly with the edge of a knife. He poured more coffee—thank God, Kate liked good coffee—and sat on a gimpy-legged chair at the kitchen table. While he ate, he read Lenny's address book, starting with the A's and plowing straight through.

"Grady Fairfield" was scrawled across most of a page, with a number underneath, but no address. Spraggue shrugged, dialed. No answer.

Kate kept the phone books in the kitchen junk drawer. "Fairfield, G." lived at 455 Solano, Napa. Spraggue dumped his dishes in the sink, dressed quickly.

Kate's old Ford station wagon was out behind the winery, neatly parked in by Howard Ruberman's Buick. Spraggue had hoped to avoid Howard, hated the thought of listening to the dire consequences of Kate's imprisonment on the grapes. But with the Volvo in the police garage, he had no choice. He sent one of the cellar crew off to borrow the winemaker's keys, stressing the "no need to disturb him."

Howard came on the run. The car keys couldn't be

found. Which pocket did he keep them in? Had he locked them in the car? How was Miss Holloway managing? How would he ever cope all alone? By the time Spraggue coaxed the old wagon into life some fifteen minutes later, he had to stifle the urge to run down Howard. Reciting lines from *Still Waters* into his portable tape recorder didn't improve his mood.

Grady's address was as slumlike as Napa got, a swath of weathered gray four-story buildings far enough from the railroad tracks for the trains to miss.

The fourth-floor-front mailbox was labeled *G. Fairfield*. Ring bell and wait for buzzer. The door was propped open with a warped board. So much for security.

The steps were narrow, the hallway dingy. If Grady was a kept woman, her standards were low.

He knocked, just in case. The feeble lock yielded easily to the two bits of stiff wire he'd snatched off Kate's workbench.

Part of the Grady mystery cleared up as soon as he opened the door. She painted. Bold abstract canvases leaned against stark white walls. Two huge red pillows and a standing floor lamp were the main room's only furnishings.

He shut the door and drew the blinds.

Searching a room containing two pillows took all of thirty seconds. He bypassed the kitchen, moved on to the single bedroom.

A double mattress rested on a wooden platform dead center, mirror overhead. A few cushions, a hand-knotted rug in washed-out earth tones, a corner full of baskets, a collection of tall grasses in colored bottles...

The heavy cardboard box with the red-and-blue ad for detergent decorating one side was definitely out of place. It was packed with men's clothing; toothbrush and toiletries on top.

"You a narc?" The accusing voice was deeper than Spraggue would have expected from the slight redhead—the hair brighter, bushier than he'd imagined.

He swallowed air and said no. For the moment denial was all he could come up with.

"You know," she continued, posing in the doorway, "you guys should really give it up. I haven't dealt in years, and if I do happen to have a personal stash, what's the big deal?"

The reason for Spraggue's temporary mental paralysis was Grady herself. Just from the way she stood, hands on tilted hips, he knew she was more than aware of her own effect; she counted on it. The Martinsons had been accurate enough in their skimpy description, but Grady outstripped adjectives. Her skin was like warm honey, so flawless it lent credibility to her outrageous hair color. She made a simple blue sundress look like it had cost plenty. His eyes kept coming back to her face. That hair had a life of its own.

She didn't seem anxious to grab the phone and dial the cops. Spraggue thanked God for her previous run-ins with the police.

"You're not the gas man," she said speculatively. "Or rent man. Or the telephone repairman. . . ."

"I'm a friend of Lenny's." Spraggue offered the lie along with a tentative smile. "And you have got to be Grady. Lenny told me you were a knock-out, but I figured the old bastard was exaggerating again."

Her mouth almost smiled at the compliment, but she caught herself. "Lenny told you to drop in any time, right?" she said sarcastically. "And you think this is a cool moment to make a move on his girl? Jesus, Lenny's friends."

"Hey, I'm sorry—"

"I thought I'd locked the front door."

"I have hidden talents," Spraggue said. She seemed like the type who'd be intrigued by a hint of outlawry. "I didn't break the lock and I did try to call first."

Her eyes narrowed. She was still blocking the bedroom door, his only exit. Spraggue wondered whether to push her aside and bolt. "What's your name?" she asked.

He couldn't risk a lie on that. No false ID. "Michael Spraggue."

"I may have heard him mention you." A frown of concentration lined her perfect forehead. Her voice stayed suspicious. "Just when did you talk to Lenny?"

"It's been months. Look, Lenny and I go way back. I'm sorry I barged in on you. I'll leave him a note, okay? Or maybe you could tell me where—"

"You don't know," she said softly. Spragague took a deep breath; she'd bought it. She was worrying how to break the news of Lenny's death, not how to get to the phone and dial police emergency.

He decided to jump to the wrong conclusion. "Don't tell me you and Lenny have split? Jeez, that man is a moron. He—"

"I don't—" she began.

Spragague ignored her. "When I talked to him the last time, he was so happy. Told me you were thinking about getting married."

"Really," she said. "He never bothered to ask."

"From the way he was hinting around, I swear I thought I'd miss the wedding. And possibly other blessed events." He let his eyes slide down to her narrow waist. "But I guess I was mistaken about that."

"Lenny talked a lot of garbage," she said angrily. "Look, let's straighten up a few things." She stared at the floorboards, said bluntly, "I had a miscarriage. Then we broke up. And— Look, why don't you come in the living room? There's something else I have to tell you. You prefer Mike or Michael?"

"Michael."

She steered him over to one of the red floor cushions, folded herself as neatly as a kitten on the other.

"Were you and Lenny really close?" she asked. "I mean, if you haven't talked to him in months, you weren't exactly like brothers."

"Hey, if you want to bad-mouth him, go right ahead."

"It's not that. It's..." She started to tell it several ways, considering various approaches. Spragague watched her eyes. She didn't seem flustered by his attention; men must stare at her as a matter of course. Whatever Lenny

68

had meant to her once, he decided, she wasn't that broken up by his death. She couldn't be and still search for the most effective way to announce it.

She finally settled on a simple show of bravery: a quiver in her lip, a hand on his, and "Lenny's dead."

Spraggue tried to get a sense of her expectations. Her eyes were wide. She hadn't quite worked up a tear but she seemed eager to ooze sympathy. He decided a suitable length of stunned silence was called for. She pressed his palm with her fingertips. Her nails were long and painted red.

"How did it happen?" he asked finally. It seemed the appropriate question, the equivalent of "Where am I" from the recently revived fainter.

Did she hesitate? For the best dramatic effect, he knew he should look away. She'd assume he was fighting back tears. But he needed to see her face.

"I'm not sure," she said. "There were rumors and then I heard it on the radio this morning. I went to the store for the newspaper, but they're all sold out." Her lip was quivering in earnest now. "The police found his body—in some car trunk or something. It's so unreal. I mean, I knew somebody who knew a woman who was killed by the Hillside Strangler, but that's different. That's removed, you know? But Lenny . . . I mean, Jesus. *Lenny.*"

"Are you okay?" he asked.

She bit her lower lip. "Yeah. Lenny and I must have split right after you talked to him. I wasn't holding any torch either."

"He leave you because of the—"

"We just weren't getting along. He was still living here, but he was using the place like a hotel, killing time until he could move in with some new lady." She put a sympathetic hand on his shoulder. "Want some tea? I make good herb tea."

"Thanks."

She bustled off into the tiny kitchen much to Spragge's relief. Maybe with her spectacular self out of sight, his mind would engage. The front door was temptingly close.

Should he take the opportunity to escape before getting deeper into a net of lies? Dammit, how could he leave when he'd learned so little? He stood up and his knees creaked louder than the wooden floor. Grady, he hoped, would assume he was about to join her. Or maybe she'd think he was pacing the floor in grief at his friend's passing. He made his way to a bureau in the hallway, jerked open the top drawer, covering the motion with a sneeze in case the drawer squeaked.

Grady kept a lot of photos of herself. Hell, anyone who looked that good ought to. He shuffled through a pack of Polaroids, came on one of a laughing Grady hugging an unmistakable George Martinson. Somehow he didn't think Mary Ellen had snapped the shutter. He heard footsteps and shut the drawer just as Grady emerged from the kitchen carrying two teacups.

"Should I put some honey in yours?" she asked. "I don't have any sugar, not even brown sugar. I'm into health foods. I've got lemon and cream."

"I'll take it straight," Spraggue said, returning to the red cushion.

"You from around here?" she asked.

"L.A.," he said without thinking. Once the lies started, they were easier than truth. As long as they stayed simple.

"What do you do?"

"I'm in the movies." And as long as you kept to as much of the truth as possible.

"Sure you are," she said.

Spraggue wondered why he sounded more convincing when he lied than when he told the truth.

"Are you Equity?"

"Yeah," he said, thankful he'd given his true name.

"Screen Actors' Guild? You have a card?"

"Sure." The SAG card impressed the hell out of her. She got very self-conscious, smoothed her hair back and sat up taller.

"I can't believe Lenny never told me about you," she said. "And him knowing I could use an in. Speak no ill

70

of the dead and all that, but Lenny was such a pain. I mean, I'm really an actress."

Sprague gave an inward shudder, but kept a smile glued to his face. So was every pretty woman within two hundred miles of L.A.

"This stuff..." She indicated her artwork, spread out around the perimeter of the room. "This is just a hobby. I was in L.A. for months, trying for a break, you know? Auditioning, cracking my neck going up against stone walls, knowing absolutely no one. I came up here for a rest. I was practically a wreck... skin and bones."

The "skin and bones" part wasn't as hard to believe as the "wreck."

"Michael Sprague," she said. "That's really familiar. Tell me what you've done."

Lenny had probably cursed him out in her presence. Or else she'd heard of the filthy rich East Coast family. Either option was about a hundred times more likely than her having seen any of his acting work. How the hell was he going to get the talk steered back toward Lenny? How was he going to walk out the door with that cardboard box?

He mentioned a few titles, dropped a few names. She was rapt, fascinated.

He asked for more tea, mumbled his appreciation when she complied. "This must be really hard on you," he said, dropping his voice. "Lenny's death."

She was an actress, all right. She saw the opportunity for the scene and grabbed it. From the moment she'd discovered his Hollywood connections, she'd been auditioning.

The scene was not half bad. This time she even got a few tears going. Sprague held his applause at the end.

"Packing up his things must have been terrible," he said.

"It was," she said earnestly. "Of course, I packed them before I knew, but even then I had this premonition I'd never see him again. And then that horrible woman..."

"What horrible woman?"

She paused to consider the best way to spill the tale. "I put Lenny's stuff in the box maybe two weeks ago. I didn't want to be reminded of him all the time. I waited for him to show up and claim his stuff, but" —a hint of a sob touched her voice— "he never did. And then, last week, this woman banged at the door and demanded his things. It was really this dramatic confrontation. The girl-friend and the ex-wife. You ever meet his ex? Alice or something."

"The blonde?"

"No. She's short and dark and kind of plump. Pretty hair, but all shoved back and tied up on her head. No makeup. No color in her face."

"Why didn't you give her the box?"

"Well, who was she to come in here like that? I wasn't exactly Lenny's best friend at the time, but I wasn't going to sic her on him. They'd had a lot of trouble, you know. Alimony and shit. I didn't want to get mixed up in anything. Maybe she was planning to hock his clothes."

"Think she'd have gotten much?"

"For Lenny's junk? Hell, no. There's nothing of value in that box. I probably should have given it to her."

"If you want to get rid of it, I'll give it to Goodwill," Sprague offered. "It must upset you to have it around."

"Would you?"

"Sure," Sprague said easily. "Did you put Lenny's mail in the box?"

"No papers, just clothes."

"I wrote him a letter a while back, telling him I might be visiting. To this address. Do you know if he got it? I'd like to think he did." Sprague's deep voice caught a little on the last words. It was one of his acting tricks. Sounded sincere as hell.

"I don't know," Grady said. "I could check. I stick all the mail in one of the baskets in the bedroom. That big round Colombian one. . . ."

They emptied it on the bed. Junk, mostly. Except for one fat envelope, addressed in a rough scrawl to Grady. No last name. No stamp.

"That's Lenny's writing," said Spraggue.

"Think I should give it to the police?"

"It's addressed to you," he pointed out. "Maybe you should call the cops. Of course, it could be personal."

That got to her.

She slit open the envelope with a silver-handled paper-knife. Another envelope fell out, together with a thin sheet covered with Lenny's straggling print.

She read it silently. Spraggue peered over her shoulder. She didn't seem to mind his closeness, leaned lightly against him. He didn't want to touch the letter. If it got to the police, he didn't need his fingerprints turning up.

Grady, baby [it began],
By the time you get around to cleaning out that damn basket of yours, either I'll have it made or I'll be down the toilet. We had some good times, right? So, in memory of those, if anything happens to me, send my Last Will and Testament on its merry way.

The enclosed envelope was sealed and stamped, addressed to Taylor and Fordham, Attorneys at Law, 55 Kearney Street, San Francisco.

Otherwise [Lenny's note continued], keep the blasted thing for me. Oh, and if I do die, call Alicia and tell her things are looking up. I left it all to her.

Lenny

10

Spraggue woke up when the stewardess assigned to the first-class section waved the menu card in his face.

"Go away," he mumbled.

"Wouldn't you like your dinner now?" The woman's voice was so nursery-school bright that Spraggue pressed his eyes shut more tightly. "Well," she continued undaunted, "I'll just leave this on the seat next to you, and whenever you wake up..." Her voice trailed off down the aisle.

Whenever— Damn, he *was* up now.

A wave of doubt swept over him. Had he remembered everything? The box of Lenny's clothes—locked up in the station wagon. The letter to Lenny's lawyer—dropped in the mailbox at the airport. The phone call to Bradley....

The memory was enough to straighten him up in his chair, open his eyes. The nursery stewardess noticed, flashed a smile. Luckily, a pair of traveling businessmen had her practically barricaded in the toilet.

He'd just called to ask a favor; reassure Kate, tell her

he'd be back in a day or two, at most. But Bradley had been full of news; the autopsy report on Lenny was in.

"Drowned," the lieutenant had said proudly, as if he'd invented the word.

Drowned. Swimming pool? Mineral bath? Hot tub? The nearest real water was Lake Berryessa, but— Spraggue didn't get a chance to ask.

Bradley wasn't finished. Not yet. "He drowned in *wine*. Some way to go, huh?"

Spraggue hadn't answered, couldn't. He'd hung up, bought a newspaper, headed for the departure gate with ten minutes to spare. Some sadist had installed a bank of phones there too. Spraggue stared at one for five minutes, then placed another call to Bradley.

"We got cut off," he lied. "Did you get a cause of death on Mr. X?"

"Not yet, but you did hear about Lenny, didn't you, before we got—"

Click. Spraggue hung up again. Screwy phone system out at the airport.

Good old Lenny, flamboyant to the end. Drowned in a butt of malmsey.... Acceptable in Shakespeare, funny in that Vincent Price spoof, but in real life...

Hadn't there been real-life cases, though? Spraggue shut his eyes, this time in concentration, not sleep. Something to do with fermentation... One of the by-products of fermentation was carbon dioxide. And during the "pumping-over" process, when the wine in the huge vats was circulated, a man stood near the top of the tank, a hose over his shoulder, pouring wine over the cap, breathing in the CO_2. Yes. It had happened at a small winery. He was sure of it now. The winemaker had passed out from the fumes, plunged down into the tank. Drowned.

But no one had found *him* stuffed into the trunk of a car.

Drowned. God, they probably had cops crawling all over the fermentation tanks at Holloway Hills. Poor Howard.

The stewardess swayed down the aisle. Spraggue hastily picked up his menu. Steak, he decided. Request it raw, get it burned.

The back page of the menu made him smile. "Wines of California," it proclaimed. Almaden, Wente, Mirassou . . . Spraggue raised an eyebrow. Leider had made the list. A dubious honor.

He ordered steak and Leider Cabernet, kept the menu.

The bottom half of the last page even included tasting notes. Leider's '75 Cabernet was described as "deliciously fruity, with a characteristic Cabernet nose, strong oak, and a faint tang of raspberries." Half a bottle of that, Spraggue thought, might dull the edge of the airline cuisine.

The wine proved just as disappointing as the food. The only reminder of raspberries was that the anonymous critic deserved one for his review. Spraggue wished he could have read the piece in its entirety. Now that he studied it more closely, there were several suspicious strings of dots. Quoting out of context, that favorite trick of Hollywood movie publicists, transforming "What a shame the producer couldn't lure some of our wonderful unemployed young actors to take over for his superannuated cast!" into "What a . . . wonderful . . . cast!"

On the other hand, maybe the wine review was perfectly legit. Maybe the airline had stored the stuff in the same oven as the steak.

Spraggue requested water. The wine had a bitter finish.

What with the usual pile-up over Logan, the plane didn't reach the gate until eleven-thirty. Spraggue blinked in the brightly lit terminal, found the closest phone, woke the assistant director of *Still Waters*.

"It's me," he said. "Where and when tomorrow?"

"Spraggue, I've been trying to reach you for—"

"Never mind. Just tell me."

"You've *got* to leave me a valid phone number! At least check in with your aunt—"

"Do I work tomorrow or not?"

"Downtown Crossing. You'll be filming there and

76

around Park Street Station. And you're gonna love this: six sharp."

"In the morning?"

"Of course."

"Thanks." Spraggue hung up.

He wound up staying at the Airport Hilton, cramming for the morning's scenes, unwilling to waste two of his possibly five sleep-or-study hours on the drive home and back. He could have sworn he hadn't been asleep ten seconds when the phone rang: "Wake-up call for Mr. Spraggue. Five o'clock." The voice was pure Boston, the accent alone enough to wake the dead.

The dead was what he felt like. Zombie film actor.

An entire army of zombies hung out at the corner of Winter and Washington Streets. The new fresh-faced excited ones were obviously PR from the mayor's office. Or insomniac fans.

Boston Police, happily collecting overtime, stopped him at a barrier. He flashed his ID and they let him park in one of the alleys normally reserved for flower and fruit sellers.

He was seized and shuffled off to a makeup trailer as soon as his feet hit pavement. A well-preserved blonde gave him a tan, ruffled his hair, massaged his neck.

"Nervous?" she asked.

"Numb."

"You ought to be nervous. Gets you up for the scene. All that adrenaline..."

Spraggue shrugged. Up for the scene he was not. He knew there'd be trouble over his interpretation.

"Mike, baby," Everod began. Spraggue cringed, but the director plowed on. "You know you're doing something very nice, very interesting, very *forties* with this. ...Now what I *want* is modern. Very *eighties*."

"It's just not an eighties scene, Everod. I told you—"

"Play with it for me, Mike. We'll shoot it both ways, run both versions in the dailies and fight it out there."

Sure, Spraggue thought, some fight.

"Don't give me grief, Mike. It's bad enough doing location stuff *anywhere*. But *here*. The light's awful. The extras *kill* the language. Christ, I told Joey we could just *build* another Boston on the back lot, but *no*. *Authenticity*, that's what he wants!"

Spraggue wondered idly what Everod's tirade had to do with the upcoming scene.

"So I want *everybody to pull together*, understand? No grief, Mike. Okay? Ready?"

Spraggue sighed.

"Action!"

So he played it modern. The first scene was the worst, the one with Karen Cameron. It wasn't Karen; he'd worked with her before, on stage, and she was a pro. It was her role, her damned soft, pleading little-woman role.

Scene One: Our Lucy (Cameron) lurks in the street just outside the stairs leading up to Harry Bascomb's (Spraggue's) office.

Harry Bastard Bascomb, hard-boiled P.I., works in a small dump over a hosiery store. He'd refused Lucy's case earlier. Didn't touch marital stuff. Might stumble across an emotion instead of a clue.

So now Little Orphan Annie waits in the rain, hoping to accost him as he passes, plead with him, invite him for coffee, exercise her feminine wiles....

Shit, Spraggue thought. She'd just try another detective. Plenty in the yellow pages. Or else she'd move out on her double-dealing husband and do her talking in court, through a lawyer.

The only chance for the damn scene was chemistry: *if* she'd been instantaneously attracted by Spraggue, *if* he felt the same. The old Bogey-Bacall magic. But when he and Karen played it that way, Everod called it old-fashioned. When they played it cool and modern, Spraggue called it unmotivated crap.

Start and stop. Roll and cut. Never would he get used to the rhythm of film, the jerky repetitive all or nothingness so foreign to stage. They did four takes of the scene, one his way, three Everod's, broke for coffee. Spraggue checked the shooting schedule: one more scene for him that morning, another late that afternoon. Between the two, time to visit Alicia Brent.

Wardrobe grabbed him, whisked him into his stunt padding and next-scene costume. Makeup ruffled his hair again, pressed her breasts very deliberately against his shoulders. Trying to get him psyched up for the next scene, Spraggue guessed.

He left the trailer, ran in place until he started to sweat, rubbed dirt on his clothes. His stunt double had already done most of the tough work. Spraggue just had to look worried and winded. He thought about the fall downstairs; the worry came easy.

The scene started with a car chase, mercifully brief, already filmed the day before. Spraggue left all car stunts strictly to the pros. Then a footrace down Winter Street, with stops to dodge flying bullets, a fistfight at the top of a little-used subway entrance, a long fall downstairs.

The chase continued down in the subway station. Spraggue jumped a couple of turnstiles for practice. Then the villain's dash across the tracks, the sudden fatal train. . . .

Bits and pieces required Spraggue's face: the close-ups when shots were exchanged, the fight at the top of the stairs. Everod and the director of photography argued over the best angle for the fall while Spraggue stared quietly down the long flight of hard stone steps. The stunt coordinator chuckled.

"You only take the first ten. Then three of my guys scoop you up and put you back on your feet. Unless you'd like to do the whole twenty-seven—"

"I'll pass."

The scene was shot like fragments of a dream, out of sequence, unreal. Makeup puffed his eye, split his lip during the fight. Harvey insisted on three takes of the fall. Then makeup added blood, dripping from a scalp cut. The bruises and aches were all authentic.

Spraggue picked up from his double at the bottom of the stairs, staggered to his feet, stumbled after the killer.

The longest shot was the fade-out, Harry Bascomb staring down at the train-mangled body of the murderer—a man he didn't hate, didn't love—but a man nonetheless, horribly dead.

"Again!" Everod called. "Get some more dirt on Mike. More blood. Some nice stuff, Mike, but this time, pull out the stops. Don't just see Dave flat on the tracks." The actor playing Dave stuck his tongue out of his bloody mouth. "See gore. See the *inside* of a man, the fragility of a man, the yolk with the shell broken—and realize how close you were to death. Okay?"

Smell is the most evocative sense. Spragque closed his eyes, concentrated on the scent of Morrison's Funeral Chapel, recreated that little back room, saw the headless man. Fluid rose in his throat.

"Roll," Everod cried.

Spragque stared at the actor on the tracks, saw the body on the mortuary table, felt again the revulsion, the need to distance himself from awful bloody reality, the—

"Cut!" Everod screamed. "Great, Mike. Beautiful."

Spragque barely heard him. But he made it back to the trailer before he threw up.

11

ALICIA BRENT'S HOUSE WAS CLOSE TO THE SEA, ONE OF six tiny cottages huddled together on a rocky Gloucester outcropping. Summer homes mostly, but the stacks of firewood piled beside the porch proclaimed Alicia's intent to stick it out for the winter. A lonely bleak season out here, Spraggue thought. Gulls circling, the low moan of the wind alternating with the booming cry of the foghorns.

He shivered in the cool ocean breeze, knocked again. He'd been lucky so far. The drive from Boston had taken just an hour and a quarter. Open roads and no cops.

"What do you want?" The woman's voice was sharp, anxious, but Spraggue recognized it. He slipped a pleasant smile on his face, hoped all the fake blood had yielded to cold cream, soap, and water. Alicia Brent's door had a peephole Howard Ruberman would envy.

"My name is Michael Spraggue," he shouted back. "Can we talk? It's important."

"To me?"

"Yes. And me. And a close friend of mine. I could explain better if you'd open the door."

"Got any identification?"

A woman after Howard's heart. Spraggue fished in his wallet, shoved his driver's license down the mail chute.

"Spraggue," he heard her mutter. "We've met, haven't we?"

"A long time ago."

That seemed to reassure her slightly, but the door stayed shut. "Look," she said, "if this is about Lenny, if it's a condolence call or—well, you might as well save your breath."

"I wouldn't bother you if it wasn't necessary." Spraggue jammed all his actor's sincerity into the eight words, shuddered inwardly.

The door creaked open. "Come in then. The neighbors have got plenty to gossip about without us shouting on the stoop."

"Thank you." He stepped inside.

There was hardly room in the vestibule for both of them. The woman retreated hastily to her right, motioning Spraggue to follow. He tried to match Alicia, this older Alicia, to Grady's description. Short, she was. Plump, maybe to someone of Grady's slimness. Her dark short hair was streaked with gray.

Alicia led him to a small bow-windowed living room, waved him into a chair by the fireplace. The springs sagged as he dented the chintz throw-cover.

Color had done as much as it could for the place. A first impression of warmth and welcome was soon replaced by one of thrift; every article in the room was chipped, mended, shabby, cheap. An old model train circling a single loop of track lay derailed on the rough floorboards. The glow from the lone lamp was dim. Alicia Brent wore dark glasses.

"Can I get you anything? Coffee? Tea?" The woman was plainly ill at ease. She fussed with the thin curtains as if she couldn't decide whether to draw them or not.

"Coffee would be nice," Spraggue said. Maybe she'd calm down given something to do.

She knelt, righted the engine. "The kids, they leave

things everywhere. Here"—she moved to the sofa, lifted a large brown-wrapped parcel from a cushion—"I'll get this out of the way. If you'd prefer the sofa—that chair's not very—"

"May I help?"

"No. Please. I'll heat up the coffee. It'll just be a minute."

Sprague got to his feet as soon as she left, stared out the window, read the book titles on the two warped shelves. He was studying the train when Alicia returned, tray in hands.

She'd not only made coffee, she'd combed her hair, tucked in her blouse, changed from terrycloth slippers to high-heeled shoes, applied makeup like a mask. She still wore the glasses.

"Cream? Sugar?" She set the tray on an open metal TV table, tried to force cordiality into her voice.

"Black," said Sprague.

Her hand shook only a little as she passed him the cup and saucer. They drank in silence. Sprague let the tension build.

"So," she began finally. "If you'll tell me why you're here—"

"How did you hurt your eye?"

"A . . . a door. One of the kids—they're so careless. I was bringing in the groceries and she just let it slam."

"Have you had a doctor look at it?"

"No. No need. A simple black eye, really—"

"And you probably didn't know a doctor in California."

The cup almost jerked out of her hands. She set it down hurriedly. "I don't understand—"

"You were seen, Mrs. Brent."

"Don't call me that." Her tone was fretful rather than angry. "Alicia's good enough. I only kept his name for the kids' sake. Now that they're older, maybe I'll change it. . . ."

"Why did you lie about going to California?"

"I didn't. The police never asked. Are you working for them?"

83

"For myself."

"Then I think you'd better leave." Her voice trembled, died near the end.

"I'm much easier to talk to than the police." Spraggue kept his tone gentle, but the threat was there.

"What do you want to know?"

"When were you in Napa?"

Silence.

"It's so easy to find out," he said. "Airlines keep records."

"I left here September ninth, a Tuesday. I meant to stay a week, but I came home a day early."

Came home Monday, the fifteenth. And Sunday night Kate had a fight with Lenny.

"Why did you come back early?"

"I was ashamed," she said simply. She pulled off the glasses, clutched them in her lap. Her left eye, fading now, was still a mass of bluish-yellow bruise. "I didn't want anyone to see this."

Spraggue waited.

"My parents sent me the plane ticket. They live in St. Helena. They want me to bring the kids and move back there. Maybe I will...now." She gulped her coffee, coughed. "I begged them to send money instead. Both my children need braces and ... But my folks are old, they wanted to see me. A neighbor was glad to take the kids...."

"It was okay at first. The valley was just like I remembered. And then I picked up some local rag, with a big front-page story, all about Lenny Brent, the bright star of winemaking." Her mouth tightened into a hard little line. "They had a picture of him, dancing with this lovely young girl." The mouth turned wistful, shook, regained control. "And I decided to talk to him, because it wasn't fair. Why should kids grow up with crooked teeth when their father's making good money?"

She didn't want or expect an answer.

"I shouldn't have seen Lenny, but I had to. I was waiting at his house when he finally drove up. Can't you see" —her hands fluttered helplessly— "I'm not the right generation for this? I wasn't brought up to it. You got married, you had kids, you lived happily ever after. I'm coping; I'm making a living now, finally; but I don't want to. I want their father to take care of our children."

"What happened?"

"With Lenny?" She laughed, but the noise wasn't warm or funny. "He hardly recognized me. He said hello and started past me to the house, and I yelled at him. I called him names I didn't even think I knew, words I must have picked up at the hospital. I wasn't even coherent. I went there to make a statement, to plead, if you like, but not for me—for the kids—and then I acted like some hysterical idiot. I couldn't stop screaming . . . until he hit me."

The room was so still Spraggue heard ticking, noticed a clock on the mantel for the first time.

"I walked away," she continued. "I got into the car. Somehow I wound up at the airport. I had my ticket, open-ended, and I left. I looked at myself in the rest-room mirror and bought a cheap pair of sunglasses. I wrote my folks to send my things."

Spraggue said nothing.

"Lenny was alive when I left. He was."

Still nothing.

"I had no reason to kill him. None. Lenny's been dead to me for years."

"Why did you ask Grady Fairfield for Lenny's things?"

She shook her head. "I don't follow you."

"When you visited his girl friend, were you looking for Lenny?"

"I don't know what you're talking about. I've been honest with you, probably too honest."

"Or were you looking for his will?"

"I think you'd better go now."

"You *are* Lenny's heir."

This time the response was a long time coming, a tentative "What?"

"Lenny named you as his only legatee."

She replaced the glasses. "Look, I can't absorb all this. I want you to leave."

85

"All right, but the police—"

"If Lenny left me anything, it's only because he was too damned lazy to change his will after we split up. But I'm grateful. For the kids."

He left her sitting on the faded sofa. "You'll be hearing from the lawyer—"

"Wait. If I call the police, admit that I was in the area, will you tell them about this?" Her hand went to her eye, gently touched the mottled skin.

"No, but I think you should."

She watched numbly as he opened the door, started to speak, stopped.

"Yes?"

"Um . . . that girl, the one in the picture, was that his girl friend?"

"I don't know. Probably."

"Well, she's lying. I've never met her."

Somehow Spraggue got the feeling that that wasn't what she wanted to say at all. But she slammed the door behind him, chained it. No footsteps. She stood by the peephole.

He turned and walked way.

Small, plump, and dark, he said to himself as he started the car. Mary Ellen Martinson.

12

Q̲UITTING, S̲PRAGGUE THOUGHT, WOULD GET HIM A HELL
of a rep in the film industry.... Still, the temptation was
growing.

Pushing the speed limit and skipping lunch had gotten
him back downtown dead on schedule. Made-up and cos-
tumed, he'd waited.

At three o'clock, Everod decided there was still sufficient sunshine to wrap up the love-on-the-Boston-
Common montage.

Spraggue grimaced, remembered with regret his promise not to quarrel until the dailies. He just played the
scenes, thankful for their lack of dialogue, grateful that
he couldn't hear the orchestral violins that would no doubt
underscore his passion. Stock shots every one. Standard
young couple clapping along with the one-man band. First
brush of hesitant hands, first shared smile, first kiss.
Spraggue felt twenty again ... and that brought memories
of Kate—and jail.

"Cut!" Everod actually grinned at him, and Spraggue
wondered how he'd make it through the film. Quitting

might screw up his career, but surely it was worse to play this easy stereotyped "love." Leave out all the real stuff—the sizing-up, the talk, the doubts, the fears. Just gaze into her eyes and sigh and fall in love. The great Hollywood bullshit.

Everod wanted more takes. Spragge pressed his lips shut and complied. Couldn't the director *see* how wrong the damned scenes were? Lucy, the client, victim of a brutal husband, and Harry Bascomb, hard-boiled private eye, weren't exactly prime candidates for puppy love. And that's what old Everod had them playing: young love in the green grass. First love, the kind that never comes again.

Kate.

She could have drowned Lenny Brent so easily, could have stood close beside him, up on the catwalk over the fermentation tanks....

The dailies were gruesome, Everod unreasonable. Karen Cameron found the scenes on the Common "cute."

"You *did* read the script," Aunt Mary reminded him hours later, near the end of a perfect dinner. Her gray eyes twinkled.

"I read tons of scripts. *Still Waters* seemed comparatively inspired."

"Has it changed?" Innocently, Mary forked a last mouthful of strawberry tart.

"How was I to know Everod was planning to treat the damn thing like Holy Writ? I've seen directors cut Shakespeare to ribbons. Why this kid-glove treatment for some hack writer?"

"I would assume the writer's last film made a great deal of money."

"Bingo," Spragge said gloomily.

Mary chuckled. "Then you are insulting a man who has his finger on the pulse of the movie-going public."

"I'd like to get my fingers on the pulse in his throat."

"There *must* be scenes you enjoy." She nodded to the

immaculate butler. "Coffee, please, Pierce. Brandy in the library."

"My favorite is the climax: Park Street Station. The murderer races across the tracks and gets mashed by a speeding trolley."

"Nonsense," Mary said firmly.

"Fact."

"There's no such beast as a speeding trolley."

"It's one of the more realistic scenes."

They drank coffee in comfortable silence. Spraggue leaned back in his chair, felt the day's tensions slowly melt. His eyes did a quick survey of the rosewood-paneled dining room, stayed fixed on the familiar Degas.

The Chestnut Hill place was his—dining room, library, and all the thirty-odd other rooms. It was part of the loot left by his robber-baron great-grandfather, chock-full of family ghosts and heirlooms. He couldn't live there; its hugeness mocked his solitude, inquired after a non-existent wife and unborn children. Alone, he rattled around like a penny in a strongbox. So Mary lived there for him, Mary with her wondrous cook, her devoted butler, her quick game player's mind, and her ticker-tape machines.

"When's your flight?" she asked gently.

"Ten. The red-eye special."

Spraggue took her arm to lead her to the library, a courtesy only. At seventy, Mary Spraggue Hillman looked frailer than she was. The red still warred with the creeping silver in her hair. She settled in her usual chair, a green velvet wing-backed job near the bow window. Spraggue sprawled on the matching couch. Pierce heated brandy, served it in crystal snifters.

"To business," Mary said, shifting gears after a single sip. "I want to help. I like Kate. I'm good at asking questions, mostly because no one takes us dithery old ladies seriously."

"I take you seriously."

"You'd be a fool not to. I'm a damn good financial adviser. Do you think Brent's wife was really holding out on you?"

"Ex-wife. She seemed uncomfortable. She kept her own counsel."

"Works in a hospital? I feel an urge for volunteer work coming on."

"Be subtle. But let me know if she's planning any sudden vacations."

"I'm always subtle when I have the time."

"And speaking of hospitals..." Spragge's voice trailed off momentarily. "Still have your WATS line?"

"Where do you want me to call?"

"Napa. Phone hospitals, clinics, every health-care facility within a fifty-mile radius, and find out if Grady Fairfield was a patient within the past six months."

"Just whether or not she was a patient?"

"What I'm after is admittance records: Was she brought in as an emergency case or scheduled?"

"Just for my own curiosity..." Mary began.

"An abortion or a miscarriage."

"Ah...I suppose I could impersonate a Blue Cross bureaucrat."

"I'll nominate you for a Tony award."

"What else can I do?"

"Get me the gossip on corporate takeovers in the wine industry."

"Simple enough."

"Pay special attention to United Circle Industries. And a Mr. Baxter. Kate says he's been nosing around, making offers—"

"On Holloway Hills?"

"Right. She said he was persistent."

"No doubt why they employ him."

"Excuse me." Pierce could have been standing in the doorway for two seconds or two hours, so silently did he open and close doors. "A collect call for Mr. Sprague. From someone named Howard. The gentleman sounds a bit—"

"Frantic? Unglued? He always is," Spragge said. "Could be anything from a stuck fermentation to a sliver in his little finger."

90

"You could take it upstairs, Michael. Or I could move to the solarium."

"I'll get it here. Stay put." Spraggue crossed the room to his great-grandfather's desk, a hunk of mahogany that hadn't been moved since the six van-men first set it in the center of the oriental rug. He picked up the receiver and slid into the leather swivel chair.

"Everything okay, Howard?"

"Is that you, Mr. Spraggue? Thank goodness. I didn't know . . . Operator? I have my party now. Operator?"

"Howard," Spraggue said firmly. "What can I do for you?"

"Uh . . . thank you for taking the call, for accepting the charges, I mean. I'm at home, you see. At the Inn. . . ."

"Any problem?"

"The police . . ." Howard's voice cracked. "The police have been at the winery . . . almost all day. Poking and prying. They won't say what they want, and I can't keep them out. They say they've got a search warrant . . . or they can get a search warrant. . . ."

"It's okay, Howard." Spraggue raised his eyes to the high-beamed ceiling.

The winemaker's next words came out in a rush. "Is it true Lenny's dead? Murdered?"

"Yes."

"And Miss Holloway's in jail."

"Kate didn't kill him."

"Of course not . . . uh . . . I didn't mean . . . What I wanted to say is . . . It's one thing taking over if Lenny's missing . . . but if he's *dead*! I . . . uh . . . I'm going away, Mr. Spraggue."

"Going away?"

"Up to Ukiah, maybe. Start somewhere else."

"Because Lenny's dead?"

"You don't understand, Mr. Spraggue. Someone's killing people here in the valley, and I'm . . . I'm too nervous to take that. I see things . . . hear things . . . Everyone looks like a killer to me, people I've known for years. . . ."

"Howard, Ukiah's no safer—"

"Don't tell me that! People are always trying to convince me of nonsense like that! Saying it's no safer in the country than it is in the city, no safer in Napa than it is in San Francisco. Saying you could get hit by a milk truck crossing the street. I'm no idiot; I know about probability. Can't you see I have to leave? Those psycho-killers—they're repeaters. And Lenny was a winemaker. . . . Maybe somebody's got a grudge against winemakers. . . . I'm in danger!"

"The police aren't even sure the two deaths are related. I need you, Howard. At least give me two weeks notice."

"Two weeks! It's not good for my health, Mr. Sprague. My heart's beating too fast. I can't seem to calm down. Not since the police—"

"Please."

"One week." Howard's voice was faint. "I'll try to give you one more week, if nothing happens. If anyone else dies, I'm leaving. My bags are packed."

"Thank you, Howard. I'll be back in Napa late tonight. We'll talk in the morning." He hung up while the receiver still yelped, closed his eyes and shook his head.

"Bad news?" Mary asked quietly.

"Can you make wine?"

"I only drink it."

"Bad news." Sprague deserted the desk, recovered his brandy and took a healthy gulp.

"Do you know who killed Lenny Brent?" Mary asked.

Sprague sat on the couch and stifled a yawn, then ticked off the response on his fingers. "Kate Holloway. Because Lenny didn't please her in bed. Number two: Alicia Brent. Because Lenny wouldn't buy braces for his kids' teeth. Number three: Grady Fairfield. Lenny wouldn't vacate her apartment. Number four: Phil Leider. Lenny ditched Leider for Holloway Hills. Number five: George Martinson. Lenny despised reviewers and they despised him. Number six: Mrs. George Martinson. She hates Lenny's guts and I'm not sure why. Number seven: Howard Ruberman. To get his job back. Number eight—"

"Lenny had swarms of enemies."

92

"It might be easier to figure out who *didn't* have a reason to kill him."

"Then it seems to me," Mary said, "that we are concentrating on the wrong aspect of the case. We ought to be delving into the other man's background, the first victim's. Perhaps he was less unpopular than Lenny. Possibly there might be only a single intersecting point in the graph of those who despised Lenny and those who hated our mystery man."

"No identification," Spraggue said. "No ID: no suspects. We can't know who hated him until we know who he was."

"Exactly," Mary said with some satisfaction. "Pierce, fetch this young man more brandy. I have always maintained that fine spirits stimulate the thinking process."

"Sleep helps, too," Spraggue said.

"Nonsense. People spend entirely too much of their lives unconscious. Four hours of sleep per night has always been enough for me."

"But you," Spraggue said, grinning, "are unusual."

"Very true, dear boy. Now, Pierce, sit down and pour yourself a glass. And let's consider how to identify a headless corpse."

13

"KATE WANTS YOU."

"Huh?"

"It's Bradley, from the sheriff's office. Did I wake you? I'm sorry—"

"Hold it. Hold it. What time is it?" Spraggue sat up and wondered how the phone had gotten into his hand.

"Almost ten. I thought you'd..."

Ten... ten o'clock Monday morning. Spraggue breathed in deeply and shook his head from side to side, hoping the sudden movement would clear it.

"Okay," he said. "Start over."

"Miss Holloway's been asking—demanding, really— to see you since yesterday. Enright's planning to ignore the request, but he's not here right now."

"How long will he be gone?"

"Wish I knew. Couple hours, I think."

"I'll be there. Thanks." Spraggue hung up the phone and looked around.

Sun poured in through Kate's bedroom window. Had he left the curtains open by design, hoping the light would wake him? Doubtful; last night he'd been too tired for conscious thought. And his subconscious had led him straight to Kate's bed, not to the guest room. Sprague raised one eyebrow and disentangled himself from the covers.

The damned muffins were rock-hard. He contented himself with a long swig of orange juice from the cardboard carton he'd picked up at the all-night grocery, washed, dressed, and took off.

"Can we talk?" he said to Bradley thirty minutes later, glancing significantly at the chain-smoking sweet-faced secretary and recalling snatches of last night's parley with Mary and Pierce.

"My office." Bradley led the way to a cubicle no bigger than a closet, with a tiny desk crammed against one windowless wall. He sat in the single chair. "Well?"

"What can I offer for a glance at the file on your headless man?"

"It's worth zip."

"I still want a look."

"If you come up aces, you tell me before you tell Enright."

"My pleasure."

"I need to rack up a few points with Sheriff Hughes."

"I'll put in a word."

Bradley stood, stretched. "Think I'll have a cup of coffee," he said loudly. Then he whispered, "First drawer on the right. Only takes me five minutes for coffee, but that'll be plenty of time, believe me. Then you'd better get upstairs to the jail."

"Thanks."

"If Enright shows up while you're in here, I never saw you. I don't even know you."

They changed places. Bradley closed the door and Sprague fought off claustrophobia.

A few sheets of flimsy paper stuck in a manila folder; that was all Mr. X's file amounted to. The Napa County Medical Examiner had thus far left blank every space on the death certificate that called for conjecture or conclusion. Notes were affixed with paper clips, stating that the body had been so badly mauled that special care was needed, special care requiring extra time. Organs and blood samples had to be sent to various Bay Area labs, better-equipped labs than those immediately available.

Spraggue rested his head on his hands, read on. What did they know about the nameless, headless corpse? An approximate age: 22–24 years; an approximate height: 5 feet, 10 inches; an approximate weight: 155 pounds; no distinguishing scars.

Armed with that scant knowledge, the sheriff's people had plowed through the state's missing persons reports, then the region's, then the entire country's. One possibility in Arkansas, but just as they'd been about to contact the family, the missing man had turned up with a tale of amnesia and alcohol breath. None of the others had even been close.

Footsteps rang up the corridor. Spraggue had the file closed and back in the drawer before the door handle stopped turning.

Lieutenant Bradley raised a finger to his lips. He barely had room to turn around. "News," he said.

"Enright?"

"Just got a cause of death on John Doe. Preliminary. Report's on the way from San Francisco."

"And?" Spraggue prompted.

"Poisoned." Bradley stared down at a three-by-five card. "Sulfur dioxide. How's that grab you?"

"As a horrible way to go."

"I think I know how it'll grab Enright. As an out. A perfect excuse to treat the two deaths separately. Which does not look good for your lady."

"Right."

"I'm betting he'll jump at some kind of chemical-dump scandal. Not our case at all, a guy ditched here from some other county—"

"By somebody who just happened to know about the abandoned wreck in my vineyard."

"Logic never stops him. You'd better get up to see

96

Miss Holloway. I'll tell Enright you terrified me, yelling all those legal terms at me."

"He won't fire you?"

"Not like he would if he found out you saw that file."

They shook hands. There was probably a quicker way to get to the jail from Bradley's office, but Spraggue went all the way outside and started again with the left-hand door.

The jail was too modern to intimidate anyone, too obviously on the third floor to qualify for dungeon status. Still, when the steel bars clanged behind him, Spraggue felt the urge to flee. He straightened imperceptibly, walked on quickly, gave his name and objective at the next pass point. The guard called down to Bradley, performed a brief but thorough search, escorted him to a tiny barracks-green room, empty except for three folding chairs and a round wooden table.

"Wait here."

Spraggue sank into a seat, tapped his heels against the metal chair rungs.

It took a long five minutes for Kate to appear, Kate in washed-out shapeless green cotton, too short for her, with her long dark hair twisted up harshly, anchored with barrettes and rubber bands over her colorless face. The female guard accompanying her wore way too much makeup, as if to stress every difference between herself and the prisoners.

"Five minutes," the guard said sharply. "And no touching," she added, too late. But when Spraggue leaned back from the kiss, the guard's wide, over-red mouth was smiling at him.

Kate jammed her hands into the pockets of her smock, ignored the chairs. "Where the hell have you been?"

"Nobody told me you wanted to see me. Not until Bradley woke me up an hour ago."

Her shoulders came down a notch. "Oh."

"Am I too late?"

"Just about. My lawyer says I could get bail in about thirty seconds."

97

"I think you should stay put."

"Then you've got to do something for me."

"What?" Spraggue said cautiously.

"Tonight, at eight o'clock, a tasting at Phil Leider's house; you have to take my place."

"I think I'd rather be in a cell."

"I'll switch. Gladly." She kept her voice low, but the intensity was electric. Spraggue wanted to touch her shoulder. The guard's heavily shadowed eyes warned him off.

"Spraggue," Kate said, "this tasting is important to me. To us. It's a horizontal blind tasting of '77 Cabernet, and we are *honored* to be included—"

"I don't know shit about the '77 Cabernet. Send Howard."

She laughed shortly. "You want Howard representing you? Howard driving everyone nutty, falling over chairs, upsetting wineglasses?"

"I see your point."

"At least *you're* presentable."

"Thanks."

"Get Howard to lend you his cellar book. All the information's there: fermenting, aging—"

"Will Howard give it up?"

"No problem. Howard's not Lenny. God, Lenny wouldn't let the damned thing out of his sight. He practically chained it to his wrist. Not even the cellar crew could touch it."

"Was it a big, tan, leather-bound—"

"Edged in gold," she said bitterly. "Did he have it clutched to his bosom when you found him?"

Spraggue wished the guard unconscious, willed her into the far reaches of the Sahara. Kate, who never cried, had turned away, her shoulders wracked with sobbing. She feigned a sneezing attack and fumbled a wrinkled Kleenex out of her pocket. When he touched her shoulder, she shuddered and flinched away.

"Kate..."

"Don't. Don't look at me. Don't feel sorry for me. I'm

okay...really...It's just this damn place...Just being locked in a cell...Talk about something else...Tell me about the crush..."

"I haven't even checked on Howard."

"Too busy playing cop." Her smile, wobbly, but game, collapsed into another flow of tears.

"I searched your room," Spraggue said slowly, deliberately. He'd never meant to tell her, but it was one guaranteed way to turn those unexpected tears to anger. Anger he could deal with.

"I thought you believed me. I wouldn't have loaned you the car if—"

"You could have had an accomplice. He could have hidden the body in the car."

"Did you search the room next to mine, Spraggue? Did you find what you wanted? Am I guilty if Lenny was my lover? Or am I guilty if I have a lover, period?" Her chin jutted out at a familiar angle. "Who taught you how to trust, Spraggue?"

"You did, Katharine, in Paris, a long time ago."

"And who let me go to Paris?"

"I didn't think I had any right to keep you away."

"And I didn't think you cared enough to keep me away." They stared at each other until Kate closed her eyes and took a deep sighing breath. She dabbed at her nose with the soggy Kleenex. Spraggue passed over his handkerchief.

"You're the only man I know who still carries a handkerchief."

"Keep it as a souvenir. You're the last woman I dreamed I'd ever lend it to."

"Haven't we had the Paris fight before, Spraggue?"

"Yeah...Let's talk about something else."

"What?"

"About us. When you get out of here."

"When I get out of here," she said firmly, after a long sniffling pause, "we've got to do something about the house."

"Remember that chateau by the Loire? The white one with the towers and turrets and gold leaf?"

"Yeah." She blew her nose loudly. "We rented horses from an old German expatriate. The silver one tried to throw me."

"You want one of those? A white castle with towers and—"

"I want the time back," she said. "I want to be twenty again."

"You weren't half as good at twenty."

Her chin came up sharply. "I got what I wanted when I was twenty. You never turned me down."

"Temporary insanity," Sprague said. "I'll make up for it when you're out of here."

"And when will that be?"

"A few more days, Kate. If I can't straighten things out by then—"

"Do you know what you're asking? I feel like some kind of animal. I walk back and forth, back and forth."

"Things are starting to move," he lied. "It won't be much longer."

"Have they found out who that other guy was? How he died?"

"Sorry," the guard said loudly, "time's up." She turned away, so Sprague pulled Kate close and hugged her again.

"His name's still a mystery," he said. "He was poisoned."

"Jesus."

"With sulfur dioxide."

Kate's face lost the tiny trace of color it had left.

"Does that mean anything to you? Sulfur dioxide? I keep thinking—dammit, it's like some light bulb should spark when I say the words—and nothing happens. It's just high school chemistry to me."

The guard stared pointedly at her watch and took Kate's arm.

"One minute," Spraggue said. "Kate, *does* sulfur dioxide mean something to you?"

She swallowed audibly. "Ask Howard," she whispered, and then she was gone.

14

A SHOWER, A SHAVE, A CHANGE OF CLOTHES—THOSE
were minimal requirements before the eight o'clock tasting. A couple hours sleep wouldn't hurt.

Spraggue stomped the brakes as a grape-loaded gondola pulled out of a driveway fifty yards ahead, resigned
himself to a 25 mph creep behind the vehicle, and, for the
first time in days, really took note of his surroundings.

The valley bustled with its annual September fever.
Mechanical harvesters rumbled across a vineyard to his
left; the chatter of a picking crew competed to his right.
The musty grape-smell was everywhere, overwhelming.
Spraggue rolled down his window, drank it in.

With crush in full swing, getting that cellar book out
of Howard's hands might be trickier than Kate suspected.

Ask Howard, she'd said. Ask Howard about sulfur
dioxide. Why? Damn it, there was *something* he should
know, something he should recall about sulfur dioxide.

Industrial accident . . . Enright would follow that trail
straight out of the county if he could. Spraggue wondered
how political Enright's decision was. Had he powwowed

with the elusive Sheriff Hughes, decided that one unsolved murder was more than sufficient for the sheriff's current term of office? That a crazed double-murderer was unthinkable? Industrial accident . . .

What the hell was SO_2 used for? Spraggue's mind veered back to long-ago chemistry classes. Making sulfuric acid. Bleaching paper? It might have something to do with refrigeration. . . .

But the smell, dammit, that sharp, biting stink. SO_2 wasn't any carbon monoxide insinuating itself into the bloodstream, lulling the victim to final dreamless sleep. Anyone breathing sulfur dioxide would know immediately, flee—unless . . .

Unconscious. Locked in. God, what an ugly, horrible, burning death.

Spraggue felt pain in his chest and realized he was holding his breath. A bead of sweat ran down his forehead into his left eye. He rolled up the window, flipped on the noisy air conditioner.

Industrial accident. And some foreman discovered the dead man, drove the corpse to the valley, dumped it in a convenient car trunk after stoving in the skull. Why? To prevent determining the cause of death? Garbage. The man's trachea and lungs would yield more than sufficient evidence. To prevent identification, then. If he could just find out who Mr. X was. . . .

He turned into the narrow driveway by the house, drove the twisting half-mile to the winery. He parked the station wagon far up, on the right-most verge of the gravel lot, so the gondolas would have easy access to the weight scales.

Just finding Howard might be tough work. The yard teemed with workers. The whine of a gondola inching up the steep driveway drowned out all but shouted words. One load of grapes had already been dumped into the stainless-steel hopper. The helical screw conveyor revolved slowly, bringing the blackish-purple bunches up to the crusher-stemmer. The smell was incredibly intense, a fact seemingly appreciated by the swarms of vinegar flies and yellow jackets. The crusher-stemmer whirred, churning tons of pulped fruit, its paddles slapping the grapes and skins through holes in the rotating drum, freeing the juice from the berries, leaving the stems behind.

Spraggue waved at a vaguely familiar young face and blared an inquiry about Howard. A smile, raised shoulders, and a glance toward the winery were all he got for response.

A disagreement broke out at the weighing station. One of Kate's assistants grasped the stem of a purple cluster between thumb and forefinger and waved it in the face of a sweating overweight man. Spraggue grabbed a cluster from a passing load, held it aloft to see if he could divine the nature of the dispute. The juice stained his fingers.

Spraggue admired the new stainless-steel fermenters in the yard, wondered how Howard had reacted to the change from wood to steel. The grape must, piped directly from the crusher along with seeds and skins, slowly filled the huge vat. No sign of Howard outdoors.

Holloway Hills Winery consisted of two huge barnlike buildings with a concrete walkway connecting the two. Spraggue hesitated between them briefly, then chose the right-hand door. More likely to find Howard fussing in the lab than messing around in the barrel-aging room or observing the quiet bottling line.

Spraggue waited until his eyes adjusted from bright sunlight to the dark interior of the winery. The outdoor hubbub subsided to a faint hum. Holloway Hills had double walls: a two-foot airspace between kept out noise as well as heat.

He could hear far-off footsteps, but he couldn't see anything beyond the stainless-steel, twelve-foot-high tank that blocked his path. Arranged in rows, the tanks made a quick survey of the room impossible; an ideal locale for a kids' game of hide and seek. Spraggue found himself reluctant to break the silence with a loud shout of "Howard!" He wanted to look around, observe the changes made since his last visit, breathe in the heady grape smell.

And he'd hate to alarm poor Howard needlessly, shake loose a glass beaker from those hapless fingers.

He moved down the aisles, counting the shining, temperature-controlled vats, coming at last to the narrow wooden staircase that led to the system of walkways overhead. He took the steps noiselessly; he'd found his observation post at last. Easy to locate Howard from eight feet up.

Kate must have relocated the small lab when the new fermenters arrived. It wasn't much, just shelves on two walls and an elbow-high workbench studded with chemists' tubes, Bunsen burners, glass pipes, and the like. Handy to have it up here, Spragque supposed, for some tasks. Pumping over the wine during fermentation, adding the yeast strains. Inconvenient for others, not that Howard would ever complain.

He stood in front of the workbench, idly picked up a pipette.

"You looking for me?" He hadn't heard Howard dash up the steps. "Joe said a man was looking for me. Uh, I'm sorry. I hope I didn't alarm you. I wasn't sure it was you."

"Hi, Howard."

"Hi." Howard looked confused. "I, uh, if you want to talk, could it wait till later? The gondolas are coming in, and I have to check every one. Can't trust the growers. Mechanical harvesters! Right down the road! Did you see them? Terrible. Terrible. Breaks up the clusters. Not to mention the MOG."

"MOG?" Spragque said.

"Material other than grape," Howard explained earnestly. "Leaves, flies, bugs, pruning shears, hats!"

"Howard," Sprague said in his gentlest tones, "Kate asked me to take over for her at Leider's tasting tonight. I have to be able to make some semblance of intelligent comment on your '77 Cabernet. Can I borrow your cellar book?"

Howard's normally pale face glowed red for a few seconds before he turned away. "I, uh, I—"

"I promise I'll get it back to you first thing in the morning. It won't leave my hands."

Howard refused to meet his eye. He squirmed uncomfortably, finally spoke. "It's uh, it's just that I don't have it with me right now. . . . But I could get it. Would it be okay if I brought it to you over at the house? Those tastings never start till eight."

"If you'll tell me where to look, I'll find it. You leave it out by the crusher?"

"No, uh, really, Mr. Spraggue, it's slipped my mind. All this rush . . . I can't remember. But as soon as it turns up, I'll bring it over. Don't worry!"

"Don't leave it too late. I have to read the thing before I show up at the tasting."

"Don't worry," Howard repeated, still staring at the floor. "Uh, Mr. Spraggue, I hope you've thought about what I've said, about leaving."

"I have. Frankly, Howard, I'm hoping you'll reconsider."

"No, uh, really, look for a replacement. I can't stay. I really can't."

"Howard," Spraggue said, "one more thing. What's sulfur dioxide used for?"

"Well," Howard said with a puzzled frown, "of course, you have to use it at the crush, to avoid oxidation. Especially in the whites. We don't use much here, thirty to sixty parts per million, that's all. Some of the wineries use more: a hundred parts per million, a hundred and fifty parts, even. You can smell it."

"That's the only time it's used?"

"I absolutely have to go now. I won't forget about the cellar book. Don't worry about a thing. It'll be there before you leave."

Howard didn't wait for thanks or any dismissing nod. He bolted headlong down the stairs.

After a moment's pause, Spraggue turned back to his survey of the laboratory workbench. Had Howard been avoiding something with his carefully downcast eyes? Or was the man merely gifted with a glance that defined the term "shifty-eyed"?

It took him ten minutes to find the box—third shelf down, right out in the open. He'd have located it sooner if he'd known what shape to look for. The yellow sulfur sticks came with a warning label, printed in red: POISON. Spraggue read the instructions: "For use in sterilizing winemaking equipment."

He replaced the sticks carefully in the box, put it back on the shelf, and retraced his steps to the car.

15

Spraggue wasn't the only substitute at the tasting.

"Jesus, the timing!" The gray-bearded man seated next to him spoke in an undertone. "You'd think they'd have canceled the damn tasting. None of the winemakers can get away! It's crazy! We didn't even *start* crushing until September sixteenth. And now, everything's coming in at once! Cabernet before Chardonnay! Crazy!"

Spraggue sipped from one of the eight long-stemmed, numbered glasses in front of him and tried to pin down the dusky taste. Number 6, he was sure, was Holloway Hills. Good wine. Almost worth sitting through two hours of yammering about foxiness and legs and tannin for. Why did wine language sound so bad, so stuffed-shirt? More to the point, why did he react to it so badly, so much worse than he reacted to medical jargon or computer gobbledygook? Probably because it was bad enough to be the goddamned wealthy scion of the robber-baron-capitalist-pig Spraggue family, without being a wine-snob to boot. Spraggue glared at the eight round small tables, the one long rectangular one at the head, all spaciously accommodated by Leider's vast living room. The gathering was almost enough to send him out to a boxing match with a six-pack under his arm. He hated boxing just about as much as he disliked beer.

By ten o'clock the white tablecloths were stained with drops of Cabernet, pockmarked with crumbs of French bread. Spraggue teetered back on two legs of an uncomfortable chair and tried to appear rapt with attention. He wasn't sure he was focusing on the right speaker.

The bread crumbs dotted Leider's fine oriental rugs, the only items in the house Spraggue could look at without distaste. Everything else was glass, chrome, or steel, with harsh angular lines set off by pinpoint spotlights. Not a single rocking chair, not a cushion. All right angles, cold metal, and neutral tones, except for the violently colored abstract paintings on the beige walls. And even they were cold—icy in their geometric perfection. One arched steel lamp, jutting across the floor, made him think of a hospital examining room.

At a signal from the head table, the bearded man next to Spraggue got to his feet, shoved his hands in his pockets, and began to recite. "The grapes came from our San Vincente vineyard. Cool location, average rainfall just ten inches a year, so we used overhead sprinklers for supplemental irrigation..."

As host, Phil Leider could have taken his place at the head table. But he preferred sitting with winemakers to sitting with critics, or so he said. Now he jogged Spraggue's elbow, snorted loud enough for his neighbors to hear: "*Supplemental irrigation!* Dammit, Brent would have been all over that guy. Great one for stressing vineyards, Lenny was. Dull as hell here without Lenny."

Spraggue murmured agreement, picked up another glass, swirled it. He breathed in deeply, filling nose, mouth, lungs. Château Montelena? Clos du Val? The bearded man settled into a monotonous drone. Spraggue thought about death by sulfur-dioxide poisoning.

Winemakers used the burning sulfur sticks to fumigate

109

the wooden fermenting tanks, that much he'd learned from the printed blurb inside the box. Or was it the aging tanks? Eight glasses of wine improved neither memory nor concentration.

He tried again. How would you use the sulfur sticks? Light a couple out in the fresh air, toss them in the tank, slam the tiny, barely man-sized gate? Maybe they'd have to be placed inside, upright, in some kind of holder. Take a deep breath, hold it, squeeze through the gate with the lighted sticks, set them up, get out fast . . . And if someone behind you slams the gate?

Could anyone wriggle through those tiny portholes carrying burning sticks? A two-person job, then. Or maybe the whole business was handled from the top of the tank. Sulfur dioxide was heavier than oxygen. . . .

Or maybe Mr. X, freshly knocked on the head, already unconscious, had been shoved into the tank.

"The wine was not fined, stabilized, or filtered." The assistant winemaker on Spragton's left raised his voice now that he was near the end of his dissertation. "We did centrifuge. Portions of the wine were aged in Limousin, Nevers, and American oak, then blended . . . 13.4 percent alcohol, 0.63 percent acid, 0.126 percent residual sugar: those are the stats. I think it's got a lot of aging potential, but I don't mind drinking it as is."

The man gave a nervous nod and sat down suddenly. There was a smattering of applause. The drunkest clapped loudest. Mary Ellen Martinson led the round.

"Brent would have approved of that, at least," Leider confided in Spragton's direction.

"Of what?"

"Not filtering the wine. Lenny was all for leaving the damn juice alone and praying to the harvest gods."

"In Hungarian?"

"Right. According to Lenny, the harvest gods didn't speak American—" A sudden rumble of conversation and a general pushing back of chairs interrupted him.

"It's over?" Spragton said hopefully.

"Without churning out the ratings? Without identifying

110

the wines? Not on your life! All this palaver's just the appetizer. What we really want are the grades, like in college. This is only a stretch-your-legs-and-yap break. The judges hope we'll get our gossip over with and not hang around after the points are given. They like to hit and run."

Sprague nodded, stood, and stretched.

But Leider wasn't through. He spread his hands in a proprietary gesture. "So what do you think?"

Just in time, Sprague remembered that the ice palace was Leider's baby. "Impressive," he said, very sincerely, wondering what other descriptive, but not unflattering, words he could follow up with. Large?

"Michael! How are you? How's Kate? Awful about Lenny..." Sprague found himself saved from a reply to Leider by a horde of vaguely familiar faces, all eager for the low-down on the valley murders. No escape.

"Great to see you again." George Martinson, one of the more long-winded judges, pumped enthusiastically at Sprague's right hand.

"Good wine, Phil," Mary Ellen Martinson yelled across the room to Leider. "Can't touch your '75, though. What did you and Lenny do that year? Sell your souls?"

"The '75 was very special, wasn't it?" Leider beamed and nodded, then walked quickly away.

"Modest bastard, isn't he?" Mary Ellen inquired of the population at large in ear-splitting tones.

"Elegantly stated, my dear." Martinson placed a re-straining arm around her unsteady shoulders. "As usual."

"Hi, there, friend of Lenny's." Even without turning Sprague knew that the soft, sarcastic voice belonged to Grady Fairfield. What the hell was she doing at the tasting? Looking at her, in a pale green dress with that flame of hair, Sprague found it easy to believe she'd been invited many times over.

"Grady," he called softly. "Wait up."

His way was blocked by a small man who snatched at his arm and held on, a man with a plump, slightly bovine

111

face. What was the name that went with that face? Steve? No. Stefan, a pretentious Stefan.

"About Kate," said Stefan urgently. "Have they released her? Anything you'd like me to do, Michael?"

Grady disappeared through an archway.

"It's under control," Spraggue said quietly. "But I appreciate the offer, Stefan." He shook hands and tried to pass.

Stefan gripped his arm, half-pulled him into a corner. "You ever see a crush like this one? Such a cold August, and now..."

Finally, Spraggue placed him. A grower, a vineyard owner. "You doing all right?" he asked.

"Me? Sure. My grapes are the finest. And I watch them like a mother. Nice sugar. High acid—" Stefan took note of Leider, moving along in pursuit of some hostly duty. "Your crush going well, Phil?"

"Fine."

"Anyone working with you this year?"

"On my own."

"Luck, then."

Leider walked away. Easy for him. Stefan didn't have his arm in a death grip.

Stefan edged closer. "Now, I want to know everything."

"There's not much I can say—"

"Not about the damned killings! I'm sorry Kate got messed up in the whole business. About United Circle, though—"

"Huh?"

"Don't play coy with me, Spraggue. I know they're interested. That guy's been crawling all over your place. And you should let your friends in on a thing like that. Those big outfits, some of them don't like to grow their own grapes. Tedious business, planting grapes. A good grower, given the faintest hint, might be able to move in quite nicely, if you know what I mean."

"Hurting for customers?" Spraggue raised an eyebrow.

112

"Not really. Leider's doing more of his own growing, of course, and he was a buyer of mine for years—"

"Forget it, Stefan."

"No deal with United Circle?"

"Never intended. Just an idle rumor."

"Sure are lots of those going around."

"Always." Sprague carefully removed Stefan's hand from its grip on his jacket sleeve. The grower seemed not to notice, so Sprague nodded and made good his escape. He strolled through the archway into the Bloomingdale's-window dining room, searching for a green sundress and red hair, smiling and greeting people he scarcely remembered. They all asked about Kate, about Lenny's murder.

He shook them off, climbed six suspended steps to another plateau of Leider's confusing multilevel domicile, scanned the floor beneath. No flaming hair. He followed a distant laugh down a narrow parqueted hallway, climbed another six steps to the screening room.

He flicked a switch to the right of the doorway and whistled under his breath as soft indirect lighting illuminated acres of cool gray carpet. In the center of the room a rectangular seating pit was delineated by a maroon velvet wall some three feet high, broken at the corners by gray-carpeted steps leading down to the pit's interior. A mirrored wall reflected the image. Heavy maroon curtains masked the projection booth, the movie screen.

A giggle interrupted his thoughts.

"It's the only comfortable spot in the whole damn house." Grady's voice came from the velvet depths of the pit. "I think I may be just a little drunk." Her voice rippled across the room again and Sprague noticed one bare foot peeping over the back of the sunken maroon sofa closest to the door. A beige, high-heeled sandal blended into the rug.

Sprague strolled a few paces across the room, positioned himself over the foot, looked down at a spectacularly bare leg.

Grady lay back among the pillows with the studied grace of an artist's model, dress hiked, one knee bent

113

high, the other leg extended over the sofa back. She smiled lazily up at him, but didn't move, didn't attempt to pull the skirt over her thighs. Spraggue thought that if the lights were any stronger or her thighs spread any wider, he would know whether or not Grady dyed her hair.

Slowly she brought her knees together, stretched one long dancer's leg full-length on the couch. Her face was slightly flushed.

Spraggue felt like a high school kid caught peeking in the girls' locker room. She noticed his discomfiture and laughed.

"What's the opposite of a voyeur?" she asked.

"A blind man."

"No. I mean the *object* of a voyeur. Someone who likes being looked at. A narcissist?"

"Exhibitionist."

"I like to be looked at," she said. One of her knees inched upward. Not as exciting a pose as the first, but one that gave an interesting view of thigh progressing to buttock, further convincing him that underwear and Grady were strangers.

"Expecting an audience?" he asked.

"Actually I thought you might try to find me."

"So you vanished."

"I opted for a more private rendezvous." She patted a fat gray cushion next to her, swung effortlessly into a sitting position, one leg crooked underneath her. "I wanted to ask if you'd found anything worthwhile in that pile of Lenny's clothes, Mr. Snoop. Any clues?"

Spraggue removed his shoes, padded down the plush steps into the pit, and almost smacked his shins on a clear glass coffee table. He sat next to Grady. She leaned against his arm.

"No," he said.

"Nothing?"

"Even less than I expected to find. Did you forget to put anything in the box?"

She pulled away, rearranged herself, chose a reclining

pose, legs splayed on the coffee table. "So you own Holloway Hills," she said.

Sprague had to turn almost ninety degrees to look at her face. "That woman who came to see you about Lenny..." he began.

"The ex?"

"Probably not." Grady didn't look surprised. Sprague wondered if she lied for the hell of it. "Do you know Mary Ellen Martinson?"

"Only by ill repute. They say her husband's turning her into an alcoholic in the hope it'll cure her of sleeping around. I *do* know George."

"If you saw the woman who came to your apartment, would you recognize her?"

"Maybe."

"Sit near me when we go back to the tasting. I'll point out Mary Ellen."

"Isn't she sitting next to Georgie?"

"No. Only judges at the head table."

She pouted, wriggled over on her right side in a manner calculated to make Sprague aware of the green dress's low neckline. "You sure you want to go back downstairs?" she whispered. "It's so boring."

"Why did you come?"

"Phil talked me into it." She grinned, ran her hand lightly along his thigh. "Let's not go back."

"What are the alternatives?" Sprague said.

"The door has a lock."

"And no one would notice our absence, right?"

"Right." One of the thin straps of the green dress just happened to slip off Grady's shoulder. Damn, Sprague thought, she's good. He was more impressed with her acting than her sudden show of desire.

He stared down at her wistfully, shook his head. Before she'd made him feel like a naughty kid; now she made him feel old. He slid the strap back on her shoulder. "They'd notice," he said. "I'm at the table with all the winemakers. We're supposed to react to the judging."

"Then go ahead."

115

"Come with me. I need to know about Mary Ellen."

They weren't quite the last guests to return to their seats. Leider, for one, followed them. Grady found an empty place at a nearby table. Sprag鍕ue craned his neck; Mary Ellen Martinson was nowhere in sight.

George was all too evident. He got to his feet, cleared his throat, and waited for dead silence. He would, if not hampered by interruptions, he said, endeavor to deliver the first four ratings, with commentary. Then he would yield the floor to his distinguished colleague from the University of California at Davis. Bottle unveilings to follow.

"Our first wine," he began, "I found quite full in body, dark in color. Not heavily tannic, but with a definite edge. A distinctive wine, with a crisp, almost minty eucalyptus..."

Spraggue shut out Martinson's voice and concentrated on more interesting matters. Like Grady Fairfield. Why the sudden come-on from Grady? Not instant chemistry; she'd had him all to herself in her very own apartment just two days ago and hadn't made a single pass. Maybe the velvet cushions turned her on. Or the fear of getting caught.

"My colleagues and I agreed that this wine was well balanced, and with a certain amount of astringency...."

Death by sulfur-dioxide poisoning... Spraggue thought of Enright combing the valley for chemical-waste dump sites. Should he clue the captain in, let him know that sulfur dioxide was used in wineries all over the valley? No. Enright wouldn't listen. There was already plenty of evidence that the two crimes were related: both bodies had been found in car trunks; both in autos belonging to Holloway Hills. The SO_2 was just one more finger pointing at a winemaker, a winery owner, a man or woman familiar with the winemaking process.

What was crucial was the identity of X.

Someone linked to a winery. Someone who hadn't been missed, who had access to wineries, no individuality, no personality... Spraggue thought back to the frantic scene at Holloway Hills that afternoon, to the nameless young man who'd pointed the way to Howard. Just one of the cellar crew . . .

One of the cellar crew . . . No. Someone would notice . . . Maybe not. The small professional cellar crew that worked practically year-round; the absence of a member of that crew would stick out immediately. But what about the crush crew, with so many temporary helpers hired just for the harvest madness? "What happened to Joe?" one might ask. "Joe? He decided to work over at Domaine Chandon. More interested in the bubbly stuff." End of conversation. End of Joe.

Spragge leaned to his right to ask Leider, but the man was engrossed in conversation. Spragge turned to the bearded man on his left.

"Where do you get your temporary help?" he asked.

"Cellar-crew kids."

"Huh?" One person at least had been listening closely to the pontifications of George Martinson. "Pardon me?"

"I was wondering where I could hire a few more cellar kids."

"Oh. I deal with the college. You get interested workers, meet the great winemakers of tomorrow. Some of them are going to come back here and toss us out on our ears."

"You mean Davis."

"Sure. Hell of a wine department. Excuse me." He went back to listening.

College student, Spragge thought. Graduate student. The age was right. The whole damn setup was perfect. Parents would hardly report him missing: safe at school. Classmates, teachers would assume he was down for the length of the crush—or they wouldn't know him at all. Beginning of the term. Not much time to make new friends or renew old acquaintances. A college student . . .

"Thanks," Spragge said to his neighbor. "Think I'll take a ride out there tomorrow."

The judges finished yapping, ripped the swaddling napkins off the bottles to exclamations and applause. Spragge

117

checked his score sheet; he'd identified six of the eight correctly. At least he hadn't mistaken Holloway Hills.

The Holloway Hills Cabernet took third place in the tasting, with a rating of 16 on the Davis scale. Good enough to cheer Kate.

Then came question-and-answer time; Spraggue fielded two, grateful for Howard's meticulously neat cellar book.

After the Davis professor delivered the final oration, Martinson got to his feet again. "Thank you all for coming," he said. "Especially at this hectic time." Guests started to shove their chairs back in preparation for departure. "One moment, please." Martinson held up one hand like a policeman directing traffic. "I just want to say that all of us in the valley have experienced a loss in the death of Leonard Brent, a winemaker of skill and knowledge. As we finish this tasting, I raise my glass, and ask you all to join me in a toast to our departed colleague. Please remain standing for a moment of silence in his memory." Martinson stood and the assembly echoed his movement.

"To Lenny Brent. Rest in peace, dear friend," Martinson intoned. He drank, then lowered his head.

The screech of a wooden chair broke the silence, followed by the determined click of stiletto heels. Mary Ellen Martinson, none too steady on her feet, walked quickly from the room.

Spraggue caught Grady's eye.

She nodded, whispered, "That's the one."

16

A HOSTILE ALARM CLOCK CLANGED AT SIX THE NEXT morning. In spite of the quarts of water he'd drunk and the aspirins he'd downed as countermeasures the night before, Spraggue's mouth was as dry as sawdust and his head felt as if it were stuffed with cotton batting. A glass of orange juice and a shower helped. A sizable group of last evening's tasters had sipped and spat into champagne coolers provided for that purpose. Spraggue hadn't followed their lead; he considered himself a drinker, not a taster.

Breakfast made him feel almost human. The ride up to Davis wasn't all that bad.

The University of California hadn't splurged on any lavish office for the chairman of the world-renowned enology department at the Davis campus. Sheriff Hughes of Napa County had a larger, more impressive one. The desk and chairs were plain and solid; the venerable Dr. Eustace might have brought them in from home. The windows behind the old man's head were dingy. Dust motes lazed in the pale rays of the morning sun.

Dr. Eustace was more than willing to help. He was a fusser, a pencil-and-paper-clip fiddler. He stepped all over himself in his ineffectual eagerness.

"Spraggue?" He considered the name while extending his hand for a desultory shake. "Spraggue! Holloway Hills! Of course. Fine wine you make up there, good stuff. I'm sure that Davis can be of assistance to you."

Spraggue forced a smile. "I'm searching for one of your students, actually," he began.

"Wonderful!" said Dr. Eustace enthusiastically. "I'm sure we can find you a hard worker, a real up-and-coming star. Unfortunately, you're late. Several of our most promising youngsters have already been snapped up. Some owners use the same students year after year. Hire them before the ink's dry on the diplomas. Never enough students for the insatiable industry. Wasn't always like that."

Finally, the professor took a deep breath enough to warrant interruption.

"I'm looking for one of your students who's already working in the valley," Spraggue said slowly.

The man's mouth opened slightly, into a questioning "Oh?"

"Do you keep a list of work-study students? Where they're employed? For how long?"

"Hmmm..." Eustace tapped the desk top with nervous fingers. "That's a problem. All our kids are matched up carefully with the situation, with an eye toward where they'll learn the most, even a view toward eventual jobs. I'd hate to tamper with the arrangements now. Very disturbing for everybody: winemaker, owner, student...."

Spraggue restrained himself from saying that the student involved would almost certainly no longer give a damn.

"This is somebody my partner worked with on a previous crush," he said. "She wants to get in touch with him, but she can't remember his name."

"Then you wouldn't hire him out from under—"

"Wouldn't dream of it."

"A student who once worked for Holloway Hills. . . .
I may be able to help you. . . ."

As he spoke, Eustace burrowed in his desk, opening
and closing a profusion of drawers, rooting through piles
of paper, stirring up dust. He resurfaced some five minutes later, triumphantly clutching a leather-bound black
notebook in his right hand.

"This is the most current work-detail book. Last year's
crush should be in here. . . ." As he leafed through the
pages, his glasses slipped further and further down his
nose.

"I'm afraid," he said sadly, "that no one went out to
Holloway Hills last year."

"Maybe he worked for someone else," Sprag07ue said
quickly. "Maybe Lavalier Cellars." Not until the name
was out of his mouth did Sprag07ue recall where he'd heard
it, remember the unremarkable wine he'd shared with the
Martinsons at La Belle Helene.

"Lavalier?" Eustace frowned. "Oh, you mean Landover Valley. Lavalier is their new secondary label. Very
confusing, all these secondaries popping up. Not sure that
I approve, either. I'm old-fashioned. I don't think any
winery should turn out a product they're uncomfortable
about putting their name on. And old Mr. Finch would
have agreed with me. Owned Landover for more years
than I can remember. Passed on now. Place went to his
daughter, Mary Ellen. She up and married—"

"George Martinson," Sprag07ue said softly, almost afraid
to interrupt the old man's meanderings.

"Right." Eustace pushed his glasses back on his nose
and looked up at Sprag07ue as if congratulating a bright
student. "The roving gourmet. Our foremost food and
wine critic."

"I didn't realize Mary Ellen owned Landover."

"She doesn't work the place herself. Not like the old
man. And I think her husband would just as soon keep
the connection in the dark. Conflict of interest, you know."

Sprag07ue nodded his head.

Eustace ran his finger down a thin-lined page in the

notebook. "Let me see. We always send a few kids down to Landover. Sandy Buford last year. Graduating in June. Very talented. And Ken Morton—"

"Either of those kids about five foot ten, a hundred and fifty pounds, slight, dark-haired, unathletic?"

"I'm afraid that doesn't sound like them."

"Does it sound like any of your other students?"

"Really, Mr. Spraggue, I have so many." Dr. Eustace closed the notebook, thrust it back into the drawer. "If your partner recalls the name—"

"How many Davis students are working this year's crush?"

"I don't know exactly ... maybe twenty. Now ..."

Spraggue tried one of the menacing stares his movie counterpart, Harry Bascomb, was fond of. "Do you have a list of those students?"

"I, uh, I can check, if you'd like." Eustace almost disappeared under his desk, came up with the black notebook again. He ran his finger nervously down a column of names, never taking his eyes entirely off Spraggue.

"I'm looking for someone dark-haired, slight, a pale complexion—"

"Mark Jason."

"Jason," Spraggue said easily. "That could be it. Where's he working now?"

"As I said, Mr. Spraggue, I really have very definite feelings about interrupting—"

Spraggue tried the stare again.

"Um." Eustace ducked his head. "Mark Jason is an observer this year, alternating between four or five places, checking out different techniques—"

"Which four or five places?"

Eustace quickly rattled off the names. Spraggue wrote them down with a sinking heart. No winery that had any connection with Lenny Brent, no winery owned or operated by any of Lenny's close friends or enemies. So much for the identity of the dead man illuminating the face of his killer. . . .

"Would the description I gave you fit more than one of the students on your list?"

"Ummmm...let me see. There's—No...You said five foot ten? Five foot ten. Dark hair...I'm afraid not."

"Does Mark Jason live on campus?"

"I believe so."

"Would you be able to give me his address and phone number, in case I have trouble reaching him in Napa?"

"Certainly!" Eustace's voice cracked with relief. Anything to get this madman out of his office. He led the way to the registrar's lair, gave hurried instructions, and departed with a puzzled frown.

Armed with phone number and address, Spragque walked a few aimless blocks, settled on a phone booth. No sense in locating 25 Delmar Heights if Mark Jason was answering his phone.

He dialed 555-1210 and waited. Six rings, eight, ten, twelve. Someone picked up the receiver.

"Hello?" A high female voice, breathless with just-climbed stairs.

"Hi," Spragque said.

"Mark! Damn you, I was starting to get *worried*!" The joy, the relief in her voice made Spragque want to hang up, shove the whole business back on Bradley. "When did you get back? Where are you? Is everything okay? Mark?"

"Please don't hang up," Spragque said. "I'm not Mark, but I am trying to find him. My name is Michael Spragque."

"Who are you trying to find?" The words came back after a pause, loaded with suspicion.

"Mark Jason. I've been over at the enology department. Dr. Eustace gave me this number."

"Well, Mark's not home."

"This is important," Spragque said forcefully. "Very important." He caught himself, softened his voice. "Have you seen or heard from Mark in the past two weeks?"

More hesitation, a slight gulp. "No."

"Then I have to see you."

123

"See me? Look, I don't know what you want, but—"

"I'll knock on your door. I'll show you any kind of ID you want. You can have a friend with you. Any conditions, but let me talk to you."

"Talk."

"In person."

A long silence this time. "Okay," came the voice finally, shakily. "Okay."

"Thank you."

"I have a class at one, so—"

"I can be there in five minutes." Spraggue almost started to hang up. "Wait. What's your name?"

"Carol Lawton. Ring Mark's apartment."

"Fine." He replaced the receiver, drew a deep breath.

His map said he didn't need the car. His shoes hit the pavement hard. Damn. Damn Kate for getting him back into the P.I. game. Damn his own curiosity. He heard Carol Lawton's eager voice and felt his stomach knot. "Stay in the movies," he murmured to himself.

He didn't have to ring Jason's bell. Carol Lawton, ill at ease, waited in the hallway of the narrow four-story building. She had a thin, heart-shaped face and a tall, gawky body, lovely eyes and a tremulous smile.

"Mr. Spraggue?"

"Miss Lawton?"

She smiled at that, nervously, unused to the formality. "Carol will do."

"So will Michael." They shook hands. She had a tiny dimple in her right cheek.

The hallway was gloomy, uninviting. "Can we talk here?" she said with a hopeless look around.

"I'd like to see Mark Jason's room."

"Not until I know what this is all about." The dimple vanished.

"We could walk around the block while I try to explain."

"Let me see some identification."

Good for you, Spraggue said to himself. Solemnly he displayed both his driver's license and his old P.I. card.

"Mark's in trouble," she said flatly. "I want to know about it."

He held the door open and she walked to the right, as if there were only one correct way to circle the block.

"Don't pretty it up," she said, before he'd decided how to start. "Just say it."

He took her at her word. "A man was killed near St. Helena. The police haven't been able to identify him. I'm operating on the assumption that he had something to do with wine, that his disappearance from the valley wouldn't be noticed, that his absence here wouldn't be reported."

Carol stopped mid-stride. "What did he look like?"

"Early twenties, thin build, dark, unathletic, five-ten."

"My God." She stumbled on a patch of uneven sidewalk. Spraggue touched her elbow and she straightened up immediately. "Mark's been gone two weeks."

"Where did he go?"

She stared at the sidewalk. "He didn't say. He was mysterious about it, mischievous, like he was going to play a big joke on somebody. I should have—" She tried a laugh, but it came out all wrong.

"I'm sorry," Spraggue said. "I don't even know for sure that it's Mark. If you'd let me see his room—"

She fumbled in her purse, pulled out a battered red wallet. "I've got a picture—"

"I'm afraid that wouldn't help much."

"My God," she whispered again. "What was it? A car crash? He wasn't a very good driver."

"I'm sorry."

They marched the rest of the way in silence, but she made no protest when he followed her into the tiny elevator.

Utilitarian. That was the word for Mark Jason's fourth-floor flat. The furnishings were student-sparse, but plenty of books lined the block-and-board shelves. A picture of Carol Lawton smiled up from a silver frame.

"I'd like to take something with his fingerprints on it." Spraggue said. "Nothing of value. A pen he used. A glass from the bathroom."

125

"Will that tell you for sure?"

"It'll tell the fingerprint experts in Napa."

She led the way through a narrow hall to a tiny bathroom. "The blue glass," she said. "He'll be mad if he comes back and—"

"I won't lose it," Spraggue said. He wrapped it carefully in a paper towel.

The phone rang. Carol ran back to the living room, snatched the receiver up, color flooding her cheeks. "Hello," she said urgently, willing Mark Jason onto the other end. Her face fell. She held the receiver out limply. "It's for you."

"Me?" He stared dumbly.

"The Napa County Sheriff's Office."

He grabbed it. "Hello?"

"Well, there you are. Who's the lady with the pretty voice?" It was Bradley.

"How did you—"

"No sweat, once I got on to Eustace. God, that man can talk."

"What's up?"

"Get back here."

"Look, I've got a real lead. I think I know—"

"Just get back as fast as you can, Spraggue. Kate Holloway should be discharged any time now."

"What?"

"You heard me."

"Yeah, but—"

"We just pulled another body out of a car trunk."

"Not—" Spraggue had a momentary vision of Howard.

"Unidentified. One of the cops says he spotted the guy hitchhiking around the place. Just found him. Changes things."

"Right." Spraggue checked his watch. "I'll be there in an hour. I'll leave now."

"Check my office for a message if I'm not in."

"Thanks."

Spraggue hung up the phone and stared blankly at the girl on the couch.

17

He didn't break any speed records on the return trip to Napa. His departure was delayed; he owed Carol Lawton some kind of explanation.

She listened woodenly, her thin features utterly composed, so much so that Spraggue wasn't sure if anything he said actually registered. She nodded occasionally, but that might have been politeness, not comprehension. She broke in on his soliloquy near the end.

"But this, this new death..." She spoke hesitantly, so softly he had to lean forward in his chair and practically lip-read. "The one you just heard about. Doesn't that throw everything off? Couldn't that mean Mark's okay?"

"No," he'd said bluntly, cruelly, not wanting her to hope.

But she hadn't really believed him.

He'd taken the carefully wrapped glass and promised to phone that evening, giving her the Holloway Hills number just in case.

To shut out the memory of that pinched, hurt face, Spraggue turned on the tiny tape recorder he faithfully kept in his pocket, recited lines and cues from *Still Waters* all the way back to the sheriff's office. He didn't memorize a single line, but it kept his mind off Bradley's new discovery.

He parked at a fire hydrant, ripe for a ticket. Kate was gone, released half an hour ago, and chauffeured home. No Bradley. No Enright. No message. Spraggue entrusted the precious glass to a sergeant, with instructions to give it to no one but Bradley. In exchange, he got the whereabouts of the latest victim: Deer Park Road.

He drove north. Just past the second turn-off for Sanitarium Road, the familiar police cars, vans, and wreckers were drawn into a huddle. It was like the discovery of Lenny's body all over again, in a daylight dream.

The police had cordoned off the area with wooden stakes and heavy rope. Sunlight glinted off tripod-mounted cameras and the chrome bumper of a red-and-white ambulance. Ten or more people, each intent on a specific task, crowded the small plot of ground—motioning, shouting, staring, scribbling in spiral notebooks. The effect, Spraggue thought briefly, was much like that of an on-location film site. The sheet-covered corpse that two men lifted onto a stretcher was real.

"Just keep on moving, buddy." The gravel-voiced cop leaned in his front window as he pulled the station wagon over onto the soft grass.

"Lieutenant Bradley's guest," Spraggue said.

The man shrugged, blew a bubble out of what Spraggue had assumed to be a huge wad of chewing tobacco. "Name?"

"Michael Spraggue."

"Keep out of the way."

"Sure."

Spraggue left the car unlocked for a quick escape in case Enright caught sight of him before Bradley.

The dark-green Buick Regal was the focus of all attention. Four doors flung wide, trunk and hood uplifted, it attracted not only the scrutiny of men with magnifying lenses, but a constant barrage of flashbulbs. The left front tire rested in a low rut, but there were no tire cuts in the turf, no sign that the driver had rocked the car in an effort to get out of the hole. The tracks were clear; the car had been abandoned. Unless it was out of gas.

The rear license plate was muddy, but legible. Sprague wrote down the numbers on the back of an old business card. Either heisted from some suburban shopping mall or rented by a John Smith or Jane Doe. Still, the car was a break in the pattern. As far as he knew, it had absolutely no connection to Kate or Holloway Hills.

A van, beige with rainbow-colored letters announcing KABC, pulled over with a screech and blocked his escape route. Sprague glanced around for Bradley, saw Enright.

At six feet four and three hundred pounds, Enright was normally hard to miss. Now, face flushed to a beet red, voice raised as he hollered instructions to his crew, he was unavoidable. Sprague ducked behind a tree and listened. Was Enright so furious because he'd had to let Kate go? Or had he been on the receiving end of a few choice comments by the elusive Sheriff Hughes?

If Bradley was anywhere around, he'd have to be over in a little tree-shaded gully. Sprague took a few steps in that direction, stopped dead when the sudden hush warned him of Enright's approach.

The huge man's complexion was an even duskier hue than before. He bore down on Sprague with giant steps. "What do you think you're doing here?" he demanded. "This is official—"

Sprague turned to confront Enright and was shocked to find a toothy grin spreading over the captain's face. Sprague looked over his shoulder and blessed KABC. They had their video-cam pointed straight at Enright. The little red light on the top was flashing.

Sprague slipped into the reporter role instinctively, knowing that Enright, this new Enright with the fatuous grin, would tell him just about anything as long as that red light gleamed.

"When was the body found?" he asked authoritatively.

A woman joined him, nodded, and shoved a microphone up against Enright's chin.

"Uh . . . we discovered the body of an unidentified young white male two, maybe three hours ago."

"How did that come about?" Spraggue asked.

"Huh?"

The woman took over, and Spraggue breathed a sigh of relief. "Did you discover the body through a routine check, or did you receive information that a body would be found?" She had dark hair and wide-set green eyes. Spraggue thought he might have seen her once on the news.

"I can't answer that at this time," Enright said, looking self-important.

The reporter wasn't thrown a beat. "Are the police considering this the third murder by the Car-Trunk Killer?"

"It has certain similarities to other homicides we are currently investigating—"

"And you feel that one man is responsible for all three killings?"

"I do," Enright said, nodding his head stiffly for emphasis. He stared right into the camera, mesmerized.

"Is there anything significant about this particular death?" asked the woman. "Something you might consider a clue to the murderer's identity?"

"Well, uh." For a moment Enright looked as if he would balk at an answer. He glared fiercely at Spraggue, willing him to go away. Spraggue smiled at the camera.

"Uh . . . we do feel that we have a motive, a clear motive in this case. With that in mind, we will now review our findings in the other two deaths. No further questions, please."

The red light went off. The woman and her crew backed off for a long-shot wrap-up. Spraggue tried to tag along.

"You," Enright whispered furiously. "You. Get back here!" His grin was gone.

"What do you mean, you've got a motive?" Spraggue decided to attack.

"What do *you* mean, barging through a police cordon—"

"Look, Enright, you're wrong on this one. This murder breaks all the patterns. Why are you calling it the third in the series?"

"Wait a minute." Enright held up a huge pawlike hand. "You're saying we've got two, maybe three separate killers who get off stuffing bodies in car trunks?"

"This one is different! You've got a car that's not anywhere near Holloway Hills. It doesn't belong to anyone connected with Holloway Hills."

"So *you* say—"

"So I say. How was this guy killed?"

"Looks like manual strangulation."

"Well, that's out of whack, too. The other killer goes in for more exotic means."

"Maybe he ran out of ideas."

Sprague wished he didn't have to stare so far up at Enright. "The victim was a hitcher, right? No connection with the wine industry?"

"Not as far as we—where did you get that about him being a hitchhiker?"

"Look, I think I know who the first victim was." Sprague hoped Bradley would forgive him. "I left a glass at your office to be fingerprinted."

"Folks at my office don't take orders from you." Enright's voice was pitched dangerously low. "I think you'd better get a move on."

"I'm just trying to point out that there *are* such things as copycat killings."

"Look, Sprague, I want you out of here. For good. While your partner was in jail, I had some sympathy for you. But now that she's free, you've got no interest, legitimate or otherwise, in police affairs."

"The first victim's name is Mark Jason. He was a student in enology at U.C.-Davis."

"Write it all up for me, why don't you?" Enright said scornfully. "And leave it at my office. No need for you to follow me around."

"Listen—"

"You want me to have some of these fine officers escort you to your car?"

Spraggue muttered an obscenity under his breath, took one more desperate glimpse around, saw no one remotely like Bradley. He had to honk at the TV van for five minutes before the driver deigned to move it the necessary two feet. He broke the speed limit driving back to Holloway Hills.

18

As he mounted the creaky front steps, Spraggue called Kate's name. He knocked three times before using his key, eased the door open with a curious mixture of anticipation and dread.

"Kate?" He couldn't decide if he was relieved or disappointed by the answering empty echo. He scanned the living room: nothing. Not even his duffel bag dumped in the middle of the rug, an unspoken order to leave.

He blew out a deep breath. She was probably up at the winery by now, assuaging Howard's myriad fears.

Automatically, he walked into the kitchen to check the refrigerator door for messages. The smudged porcelain surface stared back blankly and he realized that it had been seven years since he and Kate had used the refrigerator as their blackboard. Seven years...The discovery made him feel old.

He ran his index finger around the rim of a lipstick-stained coffee cup on the kitchen table. The inch of black liquid at the bottom of the mug was still warm.

He did a quick search of the downstairs rooms, climbed

the steps to the second floor. Behind the closed bathroom door, the shower hummed.

He knocked and the wooden door opened, releasing a cloud of steam so fragrant, so redolent of Kate, that it hit him deep in the pit of his stomach.

She wore a long white terry-cloth robe, belted tightly at the waist, with a deep V neck. Spragtue kept his eyes carefully on her face, not knowing what to expect. Anything from anger to apology, he supposed. He was never certain with Kate.

"How are you?" he said.

"Okay," she answered after a long pause. "I'm about to take the world's longest shower. They made me take miserly little two-minute cold showers in jail, and the floors were cement. And the smell..."

Spragtue inhaled. "Is wonderful," he finished.

"I'm working on it."

"Can I stay?" Spragtue asked, raising one eyebrow.

"A change of heart? You weren't interested on Friday."

"I regret it. I missed you. Besides," the eyebrow went up even higher, "jailbirds turn me on."

She made a sarcastic noise and started to turn away.

"I'll dry your back. I'm sure nobody dried your back in jail."

"There are a lot of things nobody did for me in jail."

"Kate—"

She pressed her hand over his mouth, leaned close, and whispered in his ear. "You can stay."

They kissed in the doorway until she shivered and drew him into the warm scented room. He stripped in seconds and laughed when she made her traditional remark about his Eastern lack of a tan. Her robe slipped to the floor and he traced the bikini mark low on her stomach with his index finger.

"And you," he said, "still wear the most indecent swimsuit on the beach."

The yellow-tiled shower stall was too crowded for two;

134

they'd come to that conclusion eight years ago. And ignored it. The crowding increased the pleasure.

They adjourned from the shower to the bed and made love with the easy familiarity of old lovers, tinged with the urgency of a new encounter.

When they had finished, they lay in silence for some time.

"You've loved someone since me," Kate said finally.

"What is this, *True Confessions*?"

"Did you really miss me?"

He hesitated, then answered honestly. "Not until I saw you. I try not to think about you in Boston. Aunt Mary reads all your vineyard reports. She snatches them off the tray when Pierce brings in the mail, as if the simple sight of your handwriting might unhinge me."

"Does it?"

"No," he said, flinging back the sheet and frankly staring at her unself-conscious nakedness. "It's your . . . beautiful . . . *mind* that unhinges me."

"I'll bet," she said, laughing.

"You'd lose."

"You know," she said, her palm massaging a gentle circle on his stomach, "your body can remember something, long for something, even when your mind knows better than to get involved."

"Your body has an excellent memory."

She stalled before answering, twisting a strand of her long dark hair into a tight curl. "I think it made a mistake."

"Why?"

She sighed. "There's so much background for us, Spraggue, so much context. We've known each other too long."

He smiled. "Too long to live together and too long to let each other go."

She burrowed into his shoulder and, for the moment, felt as if she belonged there.

"We've had a thousand too many battles, Michael," she said softly. "I don't think we could make a new beginning. Not another one."

135

His hand slid down her spine, went automatically to the small of her back, rubbed.

"Oh, Michael," she said, "I get so tired of explaining myself to strangers, starting over from the beginning. Where was I born and who am I now and all the wayward twists and turns in between."

"I understand."

"Who else knows me the way you do? Who else remembers the girl I was at nineteen? Who else rubs my back in just the right spot?"

"You reinvent your past," Spraggue said. "All the time, for every new friend, every new lover. It's not really lying; it's self-preservation, selective memory. Even the past changes with the years."

"Sometimes it's nice not to have to invent."

"But we do. Don't you think I have a version of our fights that's totally different from yours? Your version would hardly sound familiar to me."

"If it weren't for the winery," she said, "I wouldn't have to see you again."

"Would that make you happier? A clean break?"

"I don't know." She settled back on his shoulder, breathing evenly, and Spraggue decided that now was not the time to ask if she had killed Lenny Brent.

The phone rang. Kate gave it a reproachful look and leaned across the bed to answer.

"For you." She handed the receiver to Spraggue. "Young and female. Have I been standing in for someone?"

"Lying in," said Spraggue. "Hello?"

"Mr. Spraggue? This is Carol Lawton. I'm sorry to bother you, but I thought you might have tried to reach me."

"I haven't heard anything about the fingerprints yet—"

"Because," she said hurriedly, "you wouldn't have been able to get through. The most awful thing. The apartment..." Her voice trailed off into what might have been a cough or a sob.

136

"What, Carol? Tell me."

"There was a fire. It must have started while I was out shopping for dinner. I wasn't gone more than half an hour and the fire engines were there when I got back. Everything ... everything was ..."

"Where are you now?" Spraggue rested the receiver behind his ear and started reaching for his clothes.

"At the apartment. Not my—not our apartment. I'm calling from the superintendent's, on the first floor. The damage—it was only on the upper stories...."

"Wait there. I'll be over as soon as I can. An hour, maybe less."

He hung up, slamming the receiver down into the cradle. He pulled on one sock, fumbled with his shoelaces. "While I'm gone, Kate," he said, "stay put. Don't answer the door."

"Are you going to tell me what this is all about, or are you just trying to scare me?"

"I'm trying to scare you." He buckled his belt, ran a hand through his tousled hair.

"Why?"

"Because I don't know what the hell is going on."

19

KATE'S STATION WAGON DID A WARNING SHIMMY WHEN it hit eighty-five. Then Spraggue would realize how far down he jammed the accelerator, how tightly his hands gripped the steering wheel. He'd take a deep breath, ease up on the pedal, shake out his left hand, then his right, unclench his jaw. Ten minutes later, the car would shake again.

He swallowed hard; even his saliva tasted bitter. He'd had his chance, and he'd blown it, taken nothing but a goddamn tooth glass and a cursory glance, when there *must* have been something to find, something vital. If it hadn't been for Bradley's call . . .

He rephrased it: If it hadn't been for his own stupidity. Why leave so quickly, just to view another dead body? Even if finding that corpse meant all his theories were worthless?

He checked the rear-view mirror. No followers tonight. But anyone could have trailed him that morning; he hadn't even bothered to look. He'd behaved like some moronic movie actor who'd already read the script.

Carol Lawton sat on a flowered chintz sofa in the superintendent's living room, trying to make a go of drinking a cup of tea. Her face was composed, but her hands betrayed her. When she picked up saucer and cup together, they jiggled and clinked against each other. When she tried the cup alone, finger crooked through the dainty handle, the hot liquid made dark stains on her khaki shirt. The superintendent, a bossy buxom woman, greeted Sprague with such relief that he hurried Carol out the door. The woman probably resented missing a favorite TV show for an unwelcome dollop of real life.

They walked around the block again. Sprague longed to return to their earlier circuit, yell "Cut! Take four, scene eight!" and play the hours since all over again.

The air was dead calm; the fire trucks gone. Wet patches of sidewalk glistened. The fourth-floor windows were shattered, and shreds of blackened curtains hung limply. They circled the block again.

Carol began to talk, hesitantly at first. Then, low and fast, she poured out the story, her voice carefully expressionless. Her short walk to the grocery store. Her decision to ignore Sprague, to buy Mark Jason's favorite foods. Her deliberation over packages. Controlling her tears in the check-out line. Walking home fast, building up a fantasy: the light will be on in the window. When I turn the corner, the light will be on and then I'll know that the man was mistaken, that Mark is not dead. He's home and alive. Every word came with a step, and the story turned to a ritual, like not stepping on cracks as a child. Over and over, to herself: The light will be on in the window, the light will be on....

Instead, when she turned the final corner, the ghostly flames stopped her speechless, unable even to scream. Her two grocery bags smashed to the sidewalk. She stood rooted for a moment that seemed forever, and then her feet came unstuck and she ran screaming to the superintendent's door.

"Everyone got out all right," she said flatly. "No one was in there. Mark..."

"He didn't come back," Spraggue finished.

"No."

"Have you seen the damage?"

"I looked in the door. There's just nothing left. Nothing. . . ."

"You talked to the firemen?"

She shrugged. "They said it probably started in Mark's study. He had an old lamp. I don't think it was on. I don't know. They're going to send the arson squad around tomorrow. Look—" She stopped walking, touched his arm. "Do you think this has anything to do with . . . with what you told me?"

"I do," Spraggue said gently. "I asked before, and you agreed to show me the apartment. I was interrupted. Can I see it now?"

"There's nothing but ashes. And the firemen—"

"I know."

"They sealed the door. The fire marshal said—"

"Is there another door? A back way? A fire escape?"

"One of those metal ladder-type things. I'll show you, but I won't come in with you."

Spraggue nodded. "I'll find you a hotel room. You can wait there. Damn. You haven't had any dinner either, have you? That woman just gave you tea."

"I couldn't eat anything, really. Just go ahead with what you have to do. It's nice out. I'll sit here on the grass and wait."

"I won't be long."

She gave him a weak grin. "I'll holler if the police come."

"Thanks."

Halfway up, Spraggue thought it likely that the police would be there waiting long before he arrived. Four flights up a rickety metal fire escape, in the dark, shoeless to cut down on the racket. The project, eminently plausible on level ground, seemed stupider the higher he got. Breathing heavily on the fourth-floor landing, gazing in at the ruins of Jason's apartment, it appeared practical again.

The afternoon's barren tidiness seemed mocked by the shambles. Spraggue's flashlight, the tiny one he always kept on his key ring, picked up sodden footprints in the formerly shaggy rug. The prints gave him confidence; if a fireman had stood there, the floor was structurally sound. Carefully, he lowered himself through the window. His socks were instantly soaked. The tenants on the floor below must have been damn near flooded out.

In Mark and Carol's apartment it was a toss-up as to which had caused more damage: fire, water, or the final smashing ax searching for the last flaming hideout.

Spraggue dampened his handkerchief on the soaking rug, wrapped it around the lower half of his face, coughed. The acrid smell invaded his nostrils, seeped into his hair, his clothes.

The fire had started in the study. That afternoon, he'd sat in the living room. The archway, he'd remembered, led to bedroom and bath. That other door, to the kitchen. There: that small half-room, door crazily askew, that must be, must have been, Mark Jason's study.

The lump of charred wood in front of the small window could have been a desk. Spraggue played the pencil-flash over it, found the brass hardware on the unopenable drawers. He poked at fragments of waterlogged paper with a tentative finger. Whatever Jason had kept in his desk was a secret now and forever.

The two-drawer metal file cabinet in the corner should have suffered less damage. Had firemen opened the drawers, soaked the already burning papers? Or had the file been opened before the fire, the papers strewn on the floor, lit with matches? Maybe the arson squad could find the answer, the futile answer. The papers were destroyed.

Spraggue searched the apartment with quiet irrational thoroughness, marveling at the destruction, unable to concede defeat. He found the odd item almost untouched, by fortuitous placement or pure chance. A jewelry box was singed, soggy, but otherwise whole. Spraggue placed it carefully on the sodden bed. A stuffed unicorn was gray rather than white, even its golden horn smudged with soot, but he added it to the pile. He thought about clothes, a toothbrush for Carol, decided against them. They could be bought; no sentimental value to a toothbrush.

At the very back of the bedroom closet, an attaché case stood out in the flash beam. Spragge dragged it out onto the bed. The locks held, but the fabric gave way easily, and it opened in a way never intended by the manufacturer, yielded to reveal soggy, wrinkled papers— unburned, water-stained, possibly legible.

Spragge replaced the empty case in the closet, added the papers to the pile of salvage on the bed. He stuffed his meager acquisitions into a damp pillowcase, checked to see that he'd left the flat in its own disorder, and climbed cautiously out into the night.

Carol was cheered by the sight of the jewelry box, saddened by the unicorn. But she took them both with a simple "thank you" and held her emotions in check.

"Someplace to eat and a quiet hotel," Spragge said firmly, taking her arm and helping her to her feet.

"I could . . . I don't know . . . maybe stay with a friend. Or even call my folks."

"Do they live nearby?"

"Not really. Down near San Diego. And I guess I'd rather stick around. In case—in case Mark comes back." She bit her lip. "I know you don't think he will."

"But I *do* think it would be a good idea for you to stay in Davis. It might help the investigation. The Napa County Sheriff's Office would foot your hotel bills," he said. He'd pay the bills. In case they needed her to identify the headless corpse.

"Food and drink," he said. "Where?"

She gave him halfhearted directions to a storefront restaurant on a dimly lit side street. Most of the tables were bare formica slabs; a few boasted faded red-and-white-checked cloths. An aging flustered waiter doled out cracked leather menus. Italian food, Italian wine. Spragge ordered a bottle and waited until Carol downed a glass like medicine before he started to talk.

"I didn't find much up there," he said.

"I'm surprised you found this." She indicated the jewel case. "There's nothing valuable inside, but I'm glad to have it, as a keepsake...." She folded her arms on the table, rested her head on them, closed her eyes. "I think I'm in shock or something. I just can't believe it, that I don't have any of my things anymore, my books, my clothes. And Mark..."

"Carol, I need help. I know you're tired, and if you can't handle it now, I could wait until tomorrow."

"What?"

"I want to ask you some questions about Mark. What he was like. What he was working on."

"We didn't talk about his work. I'm not into wine-making."

"Whatever you remember will be more than I've got now. You willing to try?"

They spent some time over menus. "The lasagna's good," Carol said, "and the baked eggplant. But—"

"Not hungry?"

"I'm not sure."

"Order something. If looking at it makes you sick, we'll hide it under the table."

She ordered eggplant; Spraggue ordered lasagna. The waiter smiled and went away. Spraggue wondered if Carol had dined here with Mark Jason.

"Okay, when was the last time you saw Mark?"

She gulped and turned pale.

"I'm sorry. We can do this some other time—"

"No...No...I'll try. I'm sorry. It was a Thursday morning, I think. Yes. The eleventh."

"What time?"

"Early. Eight o'clock."

"How do you know?"

"The alarm rang."

"Usual time?"

"No. Early. So Mark could leave."

"How was he that morning? Nervous?"

"Excited more than anything. Singing in the shower."

143

"Did he give you any phone number where you could reach him?"

"No. He said he'd be traveling around, that he'd try to keep in touch. He hates it when I get possessive."

"Did he mention any winery he was going to?"

She shook her head.

"Any person, any name?"

"He might have. I don't remember."

"A woman's name?"

She almost smiled. "I don't think so. I would have remembered that."

"Close your eyes."

"Why?"

"Helps you concentrate. I'm going to say some names. If any one of them seems familiar, stop me."

"Okay. But I really don't think I can—"

"Try."

Obediently, she closed her eyes.

"George Martinson," Sprague said. "Howard Ruberman. Philip Leider." What was the guy from United Circle's name? "Baxter." No reaction. "Lenny Brent."

Her eyes flew open.

"Yes?"

"The last one. Say it again."

"Lenny. Leonard Brent." Sprague fished in his pocket, drew a dog-eared photo of Lenny from his wallet, passed it across the table.

"Him."

Sprague relaxed suddenly, deep inside. A connection after all.

"Yes?"

"Mark didn't say anything about him that morning, but that's the guy who had dinner with Mark a few weeks ago. I had a late class—summer-school finals—and I practically ran into him when I was going out the door. I was glad Mark wouldn't be eating alone."

"Mark introduced you?"

"He must have. I think he said something about Lenny

144

working at the lab. Look, does that help? Do you think this Lenny killed Mark?"

"Lenny's dead."

"Oh."

Spraggue felt suddenly drained. He needed more answers, more information, more time. The waiter brought cracked china plates, each with a tomato-sauce-covered mound in the center and a pile of salad trailing off to one side. He ate while Carol pushed food aimlessly around her dish, half-asleep, one hand stroking the soggy unicorn.

He got her registered at a hotel she knew of near campus, took a separate room for himself, ignoring the leering grin of a seedy bellhop at their lack of luggage.

Not until one in the morning did he remember the soaked papers from Jason's attaché case. He handled them carefully. Undecipherable. Except for one news clipping, a wine review. By-line: George Martinson.

20

Dr. Eustace peered inquiringly over the top of his glasses. His wrinkled forehead smoothed suddenly. "Ah, yes. Holloway Hills! Did you find that boy you were after?"

Spraggue shook the proffered hand, smiled. Dr. Eustace didn't offer, but Spraggue sat in the straight-backed chair across from his desk. The professor gave an almost inaudible sigh and abandoned a stack of computer print-out.

"Can I help you?" he said reluctantly.

"Mark Jason—" Spraggue began.

"Now wait a minute." Eustace stuck his tongue out between his lips, drummed a finger on the nosepiece of his glasses. "You're the man I got that call about yesterday. From some Sheriff Somebody-or-other. Maybe it was wrong of me to put my records at your disposal."

"Not at all." Spraggue used his most reassuring tones. "I assure you, I'm cooperating fully with the Napa County Sheriff's Office. If you'd care to call Lieutenant Bradley—"

"Bradley!" Eustace's forefinger stabbed the air. "That's the name."

"He was very grateful for your help in locating me," Sprague lied. "He thought you might be of further assistance in pinning down some details of Jason's career."

Eustace nodded sagely. "Mark Jason."

"For example, we'd like to know what his area of expertise is."

"Area of expertise?" Dr. Eustace said blankly, settling himself back in his worn leather armchair and steepling his hands on his chest. "He's a student, Mr. Sprague, aiming for that master's degree. Now I can tell you that Jason is interested in wine-making rather than vine-growing, but I don't see what business that would be of the Napa County sheriff."

"What really excites Mark Jason? What facet of his studies does he like best?"

"I'm afraid these days that what the students enjoy has precious little to do with academic endeavor."

"There must be something."

"Mark Jason," Dr. Eustace muttered. "Mark Jason..." Sprague sat up straighter. The old man had dredged up some half-forgotten item.

"Let me check this out," Eustace said mysteriously. "I might have some material for you."

Sprague waited motionless while Eustace pawed through drawers in an adjoining file room. Maybe, he thought, he could find another professor, a friend, one Jason had confided in. But Carol had named Eustace as the best bet.

The professor reentered the room cradling a stack of pink mimeograph paper. "I've got it," he said proudly. "It was the Jason boy who doled out these bits of propaganda. Idiocy. I mean, how choosy can a young wine-maker get? You rule out working for the big guns, it just lowers your chances for employment. Take any job you can and work your way up—that's what I tell the kids."

Sprague hardly listened. He'd grabbed one of the pink sheets off the stack.

147

BOYCOTT THE CORPORATE GIANTS, read the boldface headline.

All over California, small wineries are being bought up by huge conglomerates, merged into larger wineries, combined into corporate megaliths!!!

SMALL WINERIES STRIVE FOR EXCELLENCE!
CORPORATIONS STRIVE FOR PROFITS!

The headline was repeated and underlined at the bottom of the page: BOYCOTT THE CORPORATE GIANTS!!!!!!

"Jason handed these out," Spraggue muttered.

"That's right," Eustace said. "Mark hasn't gone and gotten into trouble with these little pink sheets of his, has he? I mean, with the sheriff's office involved. He isn't out trying to organize the pickers or anything?"

Spraggue reread the handout. Lenny, the great individualist, was absolutely opposed to corporate takeovers. And Leider, he'd done a nonstop monologue on corporate evil during that wild BMW ride. And Kate had refused to sell to United Circle, to that insistent man named Baxter. Maybe both Lenny and Mark had been part of some organization, some opposition to the corporations.

Spraggue stopped, shook his head. He couldn't see United Circle, Coca-Cola, General Foods sending out hit teams of paid assassins to bump off independent winemakers. Still, he wondered if Aunt Mary had turned up anything shady on that Baxter guy.

Now that his interest was piqued, Eustace stared with distaste at his pile of printout. "I don't suppose I could keep you for an early lunch?" he asked.

"Some other time," Spraggue said. "You've been a big help."

"Have I?"

Spraggue managed to extricate himself. He found a drugstore, bought a candy bar when they wouldn't give him change for the phone, stuck a dime in the slot and called collect.

148

Pierce answered with the usual runaround dodge about Mrs. Hillman's not taking any calls until evening.

"You don't recognize my voice?"

"Oh. Excuse me, sir—Mr. Michael. I'll advise Mrs. Hillman immediately. She may be angry. She's on to the exchange. I don't suppose you—"

"I can't call back later. Interrupt her. If she yells, yell back. It's good for her."

"Just a moment, then," Pierce said doubtfully. Spraggue heard his footsteps retreat down the hall. Mr. Michael! Pierce hadn't called him that since he was ten years old.

Mary's quavery voice filled his ear. "How do you expect me to keep in touch when no one ever answers at Holloway Hills?"

"Kate's probably got the phone off the hook. Reporters."

"She's free? Marvelous! You can go right on to L.A. for that film. Your assistant director's making quite a pest of himself, always calling—"

"I still need information. What have you got?"

Papers rustled. The click of the ticker-tape machine rat-tatted over the line. "More activity than I'd expected in the market, Michael. The rumor mills are working overtime."

"Fill me in."

"A major takeover by either Commercial Dynamics or United Circle. Smart money's on United Circle."

"The winery?"

"Hang on. I hope I have the names right. Landover Valley. Leider Vineyards. And you'll love this one—Holloway Hills. I may have heated up speculation by my inquiries; our connection is not exactly unknown."

"Damn."

"What, dear?"

"Grady Fairfield."

"*Susan* Fairfield, you mean."

Susan. So far Mary Ellen had been right about the pregnancy and the faked name. He wondered if she was

149

right about the dyed hair. "Go on," he said.

"A Susan Fairfield was admitted for scheduled minor surgery on Monday, August fourth, at the Spring Valley Clinic. It was one of the last places I tried, and they were very closemouthed. I hope no one fires the poor devil I finally bullied into giving out the information. Spring Valley is a very exclusive place. And very expensive."

Scheduled surgery: an abortion, then. At a ritzy private clinic. . . . Spraggue recalled Grady's cheap apartment, meager furnishings. Who had paid? George and Grady . . . ? Lenny and Grady . . . ?

"Michael? Are you still there?"

Spraggue stared at the phone. "Sorry. What about Baxter at United Circle? Did you talk to him?"

"There is *no* Mr. Baxter working for UC. Never has been. Either they're covering up or you've been lied to."

"Did you get the sense of a cover-up?"

"No. Genuine puzzlement, I'd say."

Kate. Damn Kate.

"Michael? Are you there?"

"Yes."

"Call Alicia Brent."

"What?"

"The Brent woman called here yesterday, asking for you."

"Why?"

"Wouldn't say. She'd only speak to you."

"What hospital does she work at?"

"Providence in Marblehead. Want the number?"

"Please."

More papers crackled. "It's 617-555-6718. Ask for the Dialysis Unit. If she's not there, try the house. She sounded panicky."

"Thanks."

"Take care. Can I reach you at Kate's?"

He hung up, gave his candy bar to a startled redheaded five-year-old standing just outside the phone booth. The kid scampered off in search of Mommy. For the next call, Spraggue used his credit card.

Alicia wasn't at the hospital. No one answered at home. She's in transit, Spraggue thought to himself. She's at the grocery store, at a meeting with one of the kids' teachers. Nothing's happened to Alicia Brent.

He tried the house again. No answer. The hospital. This time he got a woman who informed him that Mrs. Brent would come on duty at five that afternoon. He checked his watch. No time to waste. Too many other wisps of ideas to chase. He dialed two more numbers, spoke briefly.

The door-chimes jangled abruptly as he left the store. The station wagon sported a ticket stuffed under the windshield wiper.

He drove skillfully, but his mind wasn't on driving. He didn't notice a single scenic view.

Bradley had found him through Dr. Eustace. But how had Bradley known to check U.C.–Davis? Kate. Bradley would have asked Kate where to find him. And she'd have mentioned last night's wine-tasting. And someone, *anyone*, at that tasting could have overheard him say that he planned to visit Davis. He thought about the fire at Mark Jason's apartment. Someone obviously had overheard. Overheard and acted.

Grady. *Susan* Fairfield. She'd lied about the miscarriage all right. But what bearing could that have on Mark Jason's death, on Lenny's death? Lenny could have been the father, refused to acknowledge paternity....

No. What good was a solution that placed one piece of the jigsaw puzzle while leaving all the others scattered on the floor?

Kate. Why had she lied about a man named Baxter?

On the long ride to San Francisco, Spraggue regretted giving away his candy bar.

21

GEORGE MARTINSON KEPT AN OFFICE IN THE SAME POST Street mausoleum that housed the Wine Institute. The room itself was small, but what Martinson hadn't spent on rent, he'd more than compensated for on furnishings, from the deep-blue oriental rug to the Kandinsky lithograph over the antique mahogany desk. As Spraggue waited for the critic to finish a phone call, he wondered how much of the office decor had been purchased with Landover Valley money. Enough to keep Martinson contentedly wed to a woman who drank too much and slept around? A woman who desperately desired a memento from the estate of the late Lenny Brent. Spraggue's mind wandered back over the contents of that box—the soiled shirts, the rolled socks. What had Mary Ellen been looking for?

Martinson clicked the receiver down, flashed his white teeth. "You must have called the *Examiner*," he said.

"I thought you worked there."

"I *did*, but now I free-lance. Keeps me on the phone too much."

Spraggue nodded, drew the folded, smeared newsclipping out of his pocket. He hadn't come for small talk.

"Ah, I know!" Martinson stood suddenly, his athlete's frame dominating the room. "I have a bottle, a Fumé Blanc, just dropped off for review. Let's taste it while we chat." Martinson was already active with his cork-puller. "No, don't check the label. We'll see how good you are. I can promise you an interesting experience." He opened the top right-hand drawer of his desk, withdrew two long-stemmed glasses and an enormous white linen napkin. The napkin he wrapped around the bottle, obscuring the label. The glasses he ceremoniously filled.

"A toast?" he suggested. "Hardly 'success to crime,' eh? How about 'to Kate'? I understand the powers-that-be have given her a full pardon. *After* our most recent homicide. The valley's getting as bad as San Francisco! I attribute it to the tourists entirely. All that free tasting is getting out of hand! Why, on Saturday afternoons, you can barely crawl at a snail's pace up Route 29." Martinson's eyes fluttered nervously to the clipping. "What's that?"

"To Kate," Spraggue said. They drank.

Martinson shuddered delicately. "Needs breathing, of course." He swirled his glass, inhaled deeply, made some quick notes on a gaudily monogrammed pad of paper.

"Now, what can I do for you?" he said.

"Can't you guess?" Spraggue responded evenly.

Martinson squirmed uncomfortably in his well-upholstered gold chair. "Is that one of my reviews you're clutching?"

"You recognize it?"

"Newspaper clippings *do* resemble one another. If I could see it more closely?"

Spraggue leaned across the desk and placed the review in the center of the maroon leather blotter. He kept his hands poised, so that Martinson could read, but not touch.

"It's been rather badly kept," Martinson said.

"But it's yours?"

"I wrote it. I can make out the *G* and the *Mar*. It looks

153

old, but that may just be the care that's been lavished on it. Do you know the date?"

"I was hoping you could tell me."

Martinson shook his head. "Let's see what's on the other side. May I touch it? Thank you. If that doesn't help, I'm afraid I'll have to send you off to the public library. They have all editions of the *Examiner* on microfilm. I'm on a very tight schedule today."

"But I'm sure you can make time to cooperate with the Napa County Sheriff's Office."

Martinson pressed his lips together tightly, said nothing. He stared at both sides of the clipping, turning it carefully in strong hands. "Do you mind my asking how it got into this condition?"

"Fire."

"Oh." Martinson waited for an explanation, got none. "Can you reach the magnifying glass on the cabinet?"

Spraggue nodded, obliged.

"I can't get anything from the reverse side, but if I can pick up even a word or two from the actual review, I might . . . ah . . ."

"You recognize it now?"

Martinson leaned back in his chair. "I wish all these damned things had burned." He centered the clipping carefully on the blotter and went on dreamily. "This is the fatal piece I wrote on my re-creation of the 1979 Académie du Vin tasting. A major blow to my reliability rating. Don't smile; this is a very demanding business. Everyone *says*, 'I respect individual taste,' but then the readers *insist* that all the critics agree on the 'best' California wines. If one critic differs from the crowd, no one says, 'My, he's got an unusual taste in Cabernet.' No, sir. They say he's got *no* taste, and that's the end of that career."

"I'd like to know more about the clipping."

"But I've already told you! At that marvelous little dinner at La Belle Helene. Remember? Lettuce soup, I believe it was. Extraordinary. I wrote them up for that meal. Got a very appreciative note from the owner."

"Refresh my memory."

"I said that I'd had a row with Lenny Brent over a review." He tapped the crumpled bit of newsprint. "This is the gem that caused it. I regret ever writing it. To this day I wonder how I could have been so out of swing with the rest of the wine community."

"Out of swing?"

"I may have been coming down with a cold. Or maybe my taste buds were just off on a vacation of their own. I mean, there is such a thing as bottle-to-bottle variation, but not to that extent. And the bottle I tasted had certainly been stored under perfect conditions. I can't account for it. Lenny accused me of jealousy, and while I may have briefly, very briefly, harbored some suspicion concerning him and Mary Ellen, I'm quite sure I would never let a thing like that influence my judgment when it comes to wine."

Spraggue's right eyebrow shot up. "I'm not really following you," he said slowly. "Could you start at the beginning?"

"Sorry. I forget that you're not local. This must be common knowledge around here." He drew in a deep breath. "From the beginning. You must have heard of the French Académie du Vin tastings? Very prestigious. In fact, it was their 1976 tasting that was largely responsible for an incredible upsurge in American wine-buying. Remember that *Newsweek* article: 'Judgment of Paris'?"

Spraggue nodded. "The blind tasting where the Americans came out on top."

"Right. The French were a bit chagrined, to say the least. The market here took off. It legitimized us. Ever since then, the Académie tastings have had a special place in our hearts."

"So?"

"Their 1979 tasting was quite intriguing. A 1975 Leider Cabernet came in first, over a Mouton-Rothschild, no less."

"Good for Phil."

"Good for Lenny, you mean. *His* wine. A beauty. A huge unfiltered giant of a wine. I'd tasted it early on, from

155

the barrel, before bottling even, and I felt in my bones it would win. I predicted the entire tasting accurately in my column."

"Then why the fuss?"

"That was an earlier column. A year later I decided to recreate the '79 Paris tasting. To tell the truth, I'd heard that the *Los Angeles Times* was planning an anniversary tasting, and I thought I'd get the scoop." Martinson paused, raised his wineglass, sipped, scribbled notes on his pad.

"And?" Spraggue said impatiently.

"And when I tasted the Leider Cabernet again, right before doing that article, I was utterly disappointed. I believe I wrote something to the effect that, had the tasting been held in 1980, Leider would have been lucky to finish in the top ten. The wine had lost its bite completely. No acid, no tannin. Pleasant, yes. Mellow, yes. But a beginner's wine, a nonentity of a wine. I doubted it could be cellared. Innocuous."

"And that's what you wrote?"

"Certainly. I write as I taste. That's what I'm here for. I say what I like; the buyer can spend his dollars as he chooses. The way Cabernet prices are spiraling, you can't expect even the most rabid enophile to taste them all."

Spraggue shrugged. "I'm sure you've written unfavorable reviews before."

"But not with this reaction! Lenny *hounded* me, *embarrassed* me in public. And then the positively last straw was the *L.A. Times* tasting!"

Spraggue waited while Martinson drank.

"They praised the Leider Cabernet to the skies! I couldn't believe it! I went out and bought another bottle, of course, and I do admit that the second time I tasted it, I felt much more positive about the wine. But could I print a retraction? I'd have looked like a fool!"

"Could you write down the name of Leider's wine, the entire thing—appellation, vintage, and all?"

"Certainly." Martinson ripped a sheet of mono grammed paper from his pad with a flourish. "How do you like this wine, by the way? The Fumé Blanc?"

"Clean, crisp, slightly smoky. A St. Jean?"

Martinson unmasked the bottle triumphantly. "No. But I think it is a very understandable error. The vineyard is very close to the Crimmins Ranch. Landover Valley Fumé Blanc, 1979. You're one of the first to taste it."

"You're planning to review it?"

"Why not?"

"Does your wife still own a controlling interest in Landover?"

"You think that's conflict of interest?"

"Unless she's planning to sell out."

"Sell out? Where did you get that idea?"

"Just a rumor."

"No substance to it, certainly. Here you go." Martinson handed a slip of paper across the desk top. "Leider Vineyards Cabernet Sauvignon, Napa Valley, 1975, Private Reserve."

Spraggue read the words over twice.

"Something wrong?" Martinson inquired lightly.

"No." Spraggue tapped the memo with his fingertip. "It's just that I'm sure I've tasted this wine...."

"Yes?"

"And I agree with you completely. An absolutely mediocre bottle."

"Mr. Spraggue, that is excellent! You and me against the world! Maybe you could do a guest column for the *Examiner*? At least join me for lunch—"

"I'm sorry." Spraggue was already halfway to the door. "Where can I purchase a bottle of that wine?"

"The Fumé Blanc? I'm flattered! I—"

"The Leider Cabernet."

"The '75? I don't think you can. What little was left sold out right after the *L.A. Times* ran its rave review. When the critics speak, the people buy. I doubt you could find a bottle anywhere."

Spraggue thought he could. In an air-conditioned wine cellar at Lenny Brent's, two hours away.

22

Halfway to Napa, he pulled off at a gas station, used the pay phone. No answer at Alicia Brent's house. The hospital gave him the same routine: Mrs. Brent was due in at five o'clock. He stretched and got back in the car.

He tried the radio: scratchy AM newscasts alternated with repetitive disco wails. He tried other frequencies, finally snapped the damned thing off in disgust. Where the hell was Lenny's ex-wife? If she was so anxious to hear from him, why couldn't she stay near a phone?

He made an effort to put Alicia out of his mind, but the thoughts that took her place were none too soothing. What had Mary Ellen wanted so badly at Grady's apartment? Why had Kate lied about a man from United Circle named Baxter? Why was George Martinson so far off on a wine review and why had Lenny reacted to it so savagely? Why had Grady Fairfield made such a play for him at Leider's tasting? Why had he turned her down?

Route 29 was bumper-to-bumper, and Spraggue had plenty of time to reflect on George Martinson's dire warnings about the tourist invasion. His favorite stretch of the road, the tree-shaded cathedral near Beringer's, was practically a parking lot. He clicked on his ever-present tape recorder, recited lines from *Still Waters*, and tried to keep his temper on hold, tried to forget that tomorrow he had to be in L.A. Less than one day left . . . All those questions and no time left to find the answers. . . .

Hell, maybe he should call L.A. and cancel. Fake bronchial pneumonia. United Artists would have insurance on him; he wouldn't be hard to replace. They'd have to reshoot the location stuff in Boston. And he'd have wasted all that time spent learning to fall down stairs. . . .

Quit. And spend the rest of your life doing what? Watching Mary's investments grow? Clipping the old coupons? Maybe go back to private investigating, lifting up rocks better left unturned, telling clients cold facts they never really wanted to know. . . . He remembered Carol Lawton's childlike face, before and after he'd told her about Mark. L.A. for me, he thought. Fantasy over reality every time.

He used the same trick as last time on the approach to Lenny's. Once past slowly, scouting for police cars. Then a U-turn to park behind the bushes, hidden from the road. The lights were off, the doors locked—more than locked. Each bore a seal: *Napa County Sheriff's Office, Authorized Personnel Only*. No key under any doormat either.

Nobody had noticed the unlocked kitchen window. It was high, narrow, and a struggle to wriggle through, but at least it was around back, out of sight.

The kitchen stench was stronger. Dusty footprints outlined the path the police had followed on their search. One of the cops must have turned off the air conditioner in the wine room. Spraggue flipped it on again. He'd have to ask Alicia about the wine. If she didn't want it, he'd offer a fair price.

Spraggue breathed in deeply. The wine aroma hadn't been this noticeable before. He reached up and pulled the dangling string attached to the single light bulb.

159

The bottles had been smashed against the far corner of the wall. Deep purple stained the cement floor. Six bottles at least, maybe a dozen. Spraggue picked carefully through the shards, searching for the label, even though he knew what it would say: Leider Vineyards Cabernet Sauvignon, Napa Valley, 1975, Private Reserve. He traced the purple stain with his fingertips: almost dry to the touch. Someone had spilled the wine at least a day ago. Who? And why?

Lenny's phone was still connected. Spraggue charged the call to Holloway Hills, gave Alicia Brent's home number. She answered after eight rings, breathless.

"Of course I'm all right." She sounded surprised. "Nervous, I guess. Undecided."

"My aunt said you had something to tell me."

"I'm not really sure if—"

"One way to stay nervous is to keep everything to yourself."

"It's just that—"

"Share the bad news. It won't have to go any further. Unless..."

"Unless what?"

"Unless you're planning a murder confession."

"I'm not."

"What else could be so bad?"

She said nothing. Spraggue listened to her breathing. A chair creaked.

"Are you alone?" he asked.

"Yes. The kids are out playing."

"Then now would be a good time to spill it."

"Okay." She paused. Spraggue counted to ten. "I got a package in the mail. Mailed to Lenny, but at this address. Lenny never set foot in here."

"But you accepted it."

"Maybe I shouldn't have. I had to sign for it. The handwriting on the label seemed familiar. I don't know why I took it."

"When did this happen?"

"The day before you came."

160

Spraggue smiled grimly. That damned parcel on the couch. So that's what she'd been hiding. "Go on," he said.

"When I heard Lenny was dead...I don't know, I couldn't bring myself to open it. But then I realized, yesterday, that the handwriting was *Lenny's*. Why would he mail *himself* a package and send it here? I opened it."

"And?"

Her voice shook a little. "There's *money* in it, Mr. Spraggue. So much money that I stopped counting at ten thousand. So much money that I'm scared. How did Lenny get that money? And why did he mail it here?"

"Where did you put it, Mrs. Brent?"

"In the basement. I didn't want the kids to see it."

"Fine. Now listen. While the kids are still out, get the money and put it in a shoebox; use more than one shoebox if you have to, but nothing larger than a shoebox. Save the original box and the wrapping paper; hide them somewhere. Then seal the shoeboxes, tie them up, and call a cab. Go to a bank, not your regular bank, and rent a safe-deposit box. Put the money in there. If you need to rent more than one box, go to another bank."

"But I'll have the keys! If someone comes and—Lenny was *killed*—"

"Put the keys in an envelope and mail it to yourself. Keep mailing it until I call you, until I'm absolutely sure it's safe."

"You don't think I should go to the police?"

Spraggue thought fast. "Not yet. Just get the money to a bank."

"Okay." She hesitated a moment, then her voice came on strong. "I will. I'll do exactly what you said."

"Fine."

"Mr. Spraggue? Do you know who the money belongs to?"

It was Spraggue's turn to hesitate. "I'm not quite certain yet," he said slowly.

He sat on the bed for fifteen minutes, motionless, after he'd hung up the phone.

23

WHEN HE GOT BACK TO HOLLOWAY HILLS, KATE WAS gone. Her bed was wrinkled, but empty. The shower stall stood ajar, an irregular drip bouncing off the tile. Spraggue tightened the hot-water handle and cursed. "Stay put," he'd said. Sure.

He lifted the phone and punched the house line that rang at the winery a half-mile down the road. A kid with a lisp answered: Miss H. was not around.

Kate's purse, sitting on the kitchen counter, gave him a bad five minutes before he remembered her reluctance to drag it along, her disdain for lipstick and powder and combs. She'd have stuck money and keys in her pockets. Of course.

He carved a hunk of Monterey Jack off a slab in the refrigerator, dropped it on a chipped plate next to a pile of crackers, and sat down at the kitchen table. He ate mechanically, hardly tasting the cheese. He jumped when the teakettle shrieked.

She must have gone out to buy a paper. To get a bottle of aspirin. Any damn thing. No sign of a struggle. He opened the door, stood peering at the deepening twilight from the front porch. Called her name. Nothing.

He went inside, locked the door. The dead silence rang in his ears. he took the cellar steps noisily, much too aware of the prickling hairs at the back of his neck.

Holloway and Spragrue's grandiose plans for their wine cellar had never come to pass. The same rotting wicker furniture stood crammed in the same corner it had occupied eight years back. Two rusty bicycles mated under the stairs. Half-strung tennis rackets were mixed in with Kate's old photography apparatus. Instead of track lighting and resplendent cross-timbered, numbered wine-bins, cases and bottles were randomly stacked, elevated on gray cinder blocks, illuminated by bare bulbs.

Spragrue searched for half an hour, getting hot, dusty, and nowhere. Some of the cases were labeled and sealed: all twelve bottles alike. Some cases were mixed; those he examined bottle by bottle. He found dust, cobwebs, irritated spiders, a nickel and two pennies, but not a single bottle of Leider Vineyards Cabernet Sauvignon, Napa Valley, 1975, Private Reserve.

Spragrue swung the lid off yet another wooden crate. Probably French wine; California favored cardboard boxes. Nonetheless he lifted each bottle gently to view the one beneath without disturbing either. Jammed between the layers was a small manila envelope stuffed with 35 mm negatives.

He held one tiny strip of film up to the light, whistled under his breath, slipped it back among its fellows. He examined two more strips before tucking the lot in his inside jacket pocket. He left the lights on, raced upstairs.

Kate's purse, background before, stood out like a target now. He upended it on the table, sorted through used tissues, receipts, stamps, and old parking tickets until he found her checkbook. He sat down and studied the stubs, one by one.

He'd almost finished when the door opened.

Kate hadn't stuffed her cash in her pockets and gone for a casual stroll. The string handle of a small suede bag was twisted around one thin wrist. Its deep-purple color matched her silk shirt, buttoned just high enough to avoid arrest. She wore a cream-colored skirt, heels, even a gold chain around her neck.

She slammed the door and turned gracefully with a "hi" ready on her lips, stared at the array on the table and froze. Color rushed to her cheeks.

"You short of cash?" she asked after a moment, dangerously calm.

Spraggue closed the checkbook, rested his elbows on the table. "I was wondering if you'd been paying any blackmail lately."

"And you couldn't just ask." She unwound the purple strap from her wrist, flung the bag furiously down on a small table. It toppled off onto the floor. "No. Nothing as straightforward as that!"

"If I'd asked, you might have lied."

Her mouth set into two firm lines. "I don't lie."

"You said you'd stay here—"

"You *ordered* me to stay here! I'm not a child; I can take care of myself. And I'm already out of jail!"

"You lied about Mr. Baxter."

Her heels banged angrily as she stalked over to the refrigerator and jerked open the door. An egg teetered in its nest, hit the floor with a splat. She grabbed a fistful of paper toweling and succeeded in smearing the yolk into the floor. Spraggue waited until she'd tossed the debris in the trash, pulled an apple from the fruit bin. "I can't fight when I'm starving!" she said defensively and took a large bite.

"Did you really get an offer on Holloway Hills? Did you just make up Baxter?"

"Christ, Spraggue, of course I got an offer. And I turned it down flat. I told you—"

"Ever since I came to the valley, people have been asking me when we're selling out. The vineyard owner up the road says that a guy from United Circle practically lives here."

"Don't you have other things to do besides listen to

crap?" She reached across the table and took one of his untouched crackers.

"Kate, you're the one who—"

"I know: *I* asked you to help out. *Until I could take over again.* Your job's done. I've already been rescued, Prince Charming. Take your damned white horse and ride off into the sunset!"

"This thing isn't over." Spraggue kept his voice low and even. That irritated Kate, the shouter, more.

"It's over for *me*!" she yelled. "It's over for *you*! You're a goddamned movie actor with a shooting in L.A. tomorrow. You've got no business playing games with real life! You're not a cop, not even a licensed snoop anymore. You've got no badge that gives you any right to paw through my purse!"

"I had reasons for doing it."

"Want to tell me?" Her voice was low now, too. Cold, polite, and cutting.

"Want to tell me why there's no record of a Baxter ever working for United Circle?"

She stared down at the table. "It's nothing, Spraggue. Take my word for it. Please."

"I need an explanation."

"Crap." She leaned wearily back in her chair. "Okay, smart-ass. I'll count it out and you see if you can add it up. One: I'm an unmarried female trapped in a small-town gossip mill. Two: A very attractive guy comes by to talk corporate takeover. Three: I tell him I'm not interested in selling Holloway Hills, but I could be intrigued by other matters. Four: I get thrown in jail and my partner and sometime lover steps in. Five: I try to keep things discreet."

She reached over to snatch another cracker off Spraggue's plate. He caught her hand and held it. They stared at each other until finally, uncharacteristically, Kate looked away.

"I should have known," Spraggue said flatly.

"Known what? What the hell could you have known?"

"You're not selling out to United Circle."

"Brilliant deduction."

"You're sleeping with them."

Kate pulled her hand away. "Not the whole damned company."

"What's his name when it's not Baxter?"

"None of your business."

"None of my business! The entire New York Stock Exchange thinks Holloway Hills is up for grabs."

"David Murray," she said angrily. "His divorce decree is not final, and there are children involved."

"Did you wreck his happy home?"

"Go ahead and ask, Spraggue."

"Ask what?"

"Did I sleep with him today. That's what you want to know, isn't it? Whether I went straight from your arms to his."

"Did you?"

"What difference does it make?"

"I thought you slept around to hurt me."

"Once upon a time I might have," she said. "To let you know I wasn't exactly content to come in after your acting and your aunt and your family obligations. But it's been a long time since wounding you was the focus of my life . . . or loving you."

"You didn't have to sleep with me," Spraggue said.

"I wanted you. I thought you wanted me."

"I did."

"Just not for the long run." She rested her elbow on the table, her chin on her hand, and stared up at him from under dark silky lashes.

Spraggue crumbled a cracker to pieces in his hand. "I ought to be relieved," he said.

"Why?"

"This takes you out of the murder sweepstakes."

"But you're not relieved?"

"No."

"Have you thought about splitting?" she asked. "Selling half the winery, making that clean break?"

"I've thought about it."

166

"And?"

Spraggue shook his head no.

"Too good an investment?" she said with the beginning of a faint smile.

"Yeah."

Their hands met across the tabletop.

"Do you want a cup of tea?" Spraggue said after a long pause broken only by Kate's straightening up and blowing her nose on one of the tissues lying on the table.

She nodded. On the way to the stove, he pressed a kiss on her forehead.

"Brotherly affection?" she asked.

"The relief is starting to set in."

They held each other until the kettle sang.

"Now what's all this about?" she asked, indicating the scattered contents of her purse. "What about blackmail?"

Spraggue sat back down at the table, sipped from his steaming mug. "Alicia Brent found over ten thousand dollars in a box Lenny sent her just before he died."

"I never paid him anything but his salary."

"I found these in the cellar." Spraggue reached for the manila envelope.

"What—" Kate began.

The phone jangled. Kate's outstretched hand went to her mouth. She turned to him with a look of alarm.

"Dammit, Spraggue, I forgot. I've got messages. There were so many calls, and then coming in like that and seeing you searching my stuff—"

"Shhhhh." Spraggue picked up the receiver.

Captain Enright's unfriendly tenor came over the wire. "Finally home, Mr. Spraggue? Good. I'm sending a car right over to get you."

"Relax, Captain." Spraggue turned away from a frantically signaling Kate. "You want me, I'm on my way. I was hoping you'd appreciate those fingerprints I brought you."

"I'll appreciate them a damn sight more when I know exactly where they came from."

"A match?"

Enright hesitated a fraction of a second, lowered his voice. "Yeah. Now get over here."

So much for Mark Jason, Spraggue thought. He asked, "Have you identified your third victim yet?"

"We've got a tentative. We've turned up a wallet with some promising ID."

"Did he have anything to do with wine?"

"Wine?"

"Did he work at a winery?"

"If the wallet's his, he was just passing through. San Diego on the way to Seattle. Look, can I trust you to get here on your own?"

"I'm on my way."

"Good-bye, then."

Spraggue stared at the receiver, then at Kate. "Enright's getting polite. Is that a bad sign?"

"He sure wasn't polite when he called before."

"Were you?"

"Rude, more like it. Maybe he's getting some pressure from old Sheriff Hughes. Rumor has it Hughes may come out of hiding and take over the whole investigation."

"No need," Spraggue said absently.

"Then it's solved?"

"Messages," Spraggue reminded her. "Was Enright the only caller?"

"The phone rang constantly. One of the reasons I fled."

Spraggue surveyed her outfit. "And 'Mr. Baxter'?"

"The other reason."

"Who called?"

"Enright wants you at the station. Your assistant director needs you in L.A."

"Not until tomorrow."

"He kept muttering about costumes and publicity stills."

"Anyone else?"

Kate wrinkled her brow. "A Carol Lawton said to tell you that Jason worked in the valley last Christmas break. She's not sure where, but he stayed at the Calistoga Inn."

Like Howard, Spraggue thought.

168

"And," Kate continued, "Miss Grady Fairfield called. She wants to go to bed with you."

Spraggue's eyebrow shot up. "That's what she told you?"

"She didn't have to. I got the definite feeling that she'd just learned that you're a real-live movie star."

Spraggue groaned.

"She's out to use your body to further her career. Be warned." Kate sighed. "Damned nice body, though."

Spraggue placed his packet of negatives in the center of the kitchen table. "Very nice," he said under his breath. "Kate, do you still do your own printing?"

"Not for ages. I've got a darkroom, though."

"Look, I'd rather not give these to the police until I know exactly what's on them."

"If it's a rush job, I'll have to pass. I'm delinquent at the winery."

"Howard can handle things."

"Howard's gone."

Howard's gone. Spraggue's lips moved but no sound came out.

"Some job you did rehiring him," Kate said sarcastically.

"When did he go?"

Kate looked up sharply, puzzled. "Why so intense?"

"When did he go?" Spraggue repeated.

"About noon. He said he'd talked it over with you."

Spraggue paced the length of the kitchen twice, ran a quick jet of hot water over the dirty dishes in the sink. "Kate." He dried his hands on a rag of a towel, placed them on her shoulders. "Listen carefully. Forget the wine for tonight. The cellar crew can take it. Print the negatives. Don't say anything about them to anyone."

"Okay."

"As soon as I leave, call Enright and tell him Howard's gone."

"But . . . aren't you heading for the sheriff's office?"

"Sure." Spraggue opened the front door and stepped out into the gloom. "But first I have to stop off for a bottle of wine."

24

HE DRONED HARRY BASCOMB'S LINES INTO THE TAPE recorder all the way up to Calistoga. Turned left into Tubbs Lane automatically, right on Bennett, then slowed to a crawl. Twice he thought he must have passed the tiny sign.

LEIDER VINEYARDS. NO TOURS. NO TASTING. NO SALES. The placard wasn't more than a single foot square, faded and tilted on its post. Spraggue hit the brakes, backed up to negotiate the sharp turn into the narrow rutted driveway. The gravel track ascended steeply. Spraggue shoved the station wagon into low gear. He'd forgotten how isolated Leider's winery was, way up in the Mount St. Helena foothills far from his new Yountville home. No tourist problems at this end of the valley; Leider hardly needed the discouraging sign.

A frown furrowed Spraggue's forehead. It was just past seven; the sun teetered over the western hills. But during crush every winery kept fanatic hours. Leider's parking lot was empty.

The scuffle of his feet on the gravel seemed loud in the

stillness. The main doors were locked, the bell out of order. Spraggue started a circuit of the main building. A place that big had to have more than one door.

One of the oldest wineries in the valley, Leider's pre-dated prohibition and then some. The massive stucco château was three stories high, the way they built them back then, so gravity could do its part in the wine-making process. The facade was worn to a rich creamy yellow, the brown accent paint streaked with gray gravel dust. Circling the building, Spraggue was struck by its down-and-out air.

Around back, a broken window hadn't been fixed or even sealed. The crusher was bone dry, cobwebs in the bottom. An old crusher—probably Leider had a new one around the other side.

But the very air smelled wrong: grass, trees, late-blooming flowers . . . No heavy scent of grape must. No purple stains on the gravel approach. No gondolas ready to roll first thing in the morning.

Puzzlement increased Spraggue's determination. He passed two doors, both bolted. The third door was smaller, with a lock so trivial that, after a moment's fumbling, Spraggue found himself inside.

He closed the door quickly, leaned against its cool surface, let his eyes get used to the dim interior while he breathed in the winery's fragrance. No harsh smell of new wine; just the gentle bouquet of wine aging in old oak. He pulled his key ring from his pocket, removed the pencil flash, flicked it on.

The floorboards, old and wide, worn satiny with years, creaked under his feet. He passed through a forest of tall fermentation tanks, jacketed stainless-steel giants and smaller redwood tanks together. Out of habit, he checked the tags, the labels fastened to the tiny manholes that spelled out exactly what wine was within, what vineyard it hailed from, what temperature it was kept at, how long it had fermented. Blank. He banged on the side of one tank. An empty echo rolled back.

He passed the centrifuge, the bladder press, both dry

172

and silent. He climbed a few steps, flashed his light along the narrow catwalk, up at the great wooden beams of the ceiling. Spiderwebs. He circled the dusty floor once, then mounted the broad central wooden steps up to the second floor.

The aging room was cool, with stacks and stacks of small cooperage piled up to the high ceiling. The barrels formed a mountain, peaking far out of sight. Over to the right stood a row of huge German ovals. Spragque ran a hand admiringly along one barrel, checked for a tag, found none. A fine cask, practically new, imported Limousin oak. He found the bung, carefully removed it: empty. He tapped several others: hollow.

The pile of cardboard cartons way across the room caught his eye only because it was under one of the rare high windows, a dirty rectangle of glass that caught the last beams of the fading sun. A tarp obscured the lowest crates. He lifted it.

"I doubt you could find a bottle anywhere." The sudden memory of George Martinson's parting words was so vivid that Spragque whispered them aloud. Beneath the tarpaulin huddled case after case, all labeled: *Leider Vineyards Cabernet Sauvignon, Napa Valley, 1975, Private Reserve*. Each case had a sticker slapped on the side: *1979 Grand Prize Winner, L'Académie du Vin Tasting, Paris, France*.

His key-ring corkscrew was old-fashioned, adequate. Spragque ripped open a carton, freed a bottle from its corrugated cardboard cocoon, knelt on the floor to open it.

The cork slid out smoothly. Spragque pressed his nose against the bottle top, inhaled. He looked around for a glass, a cup, tilted the bottle to his mouth, drank. He sloshed a sipful of wine around his mouth, spat it out on the wooden floor.

His mind was still clicking, still sorting and revising, when he heard the main doors yawn open downstairs, then clang shut. He replaced the open bottle in the case, covered it with the tarp. Cautiously, he made his way to the very back of the cavernous room, behind the barrel mountain, his rubber-soled shoes almost silent on the treacherous floorboards.

Downstairs, the footsteps were heavy; no effort was made to stifle their pounding rhythm. They traced a slow, determined circuit around the periphery of the fermentation room, strolled up and down each row of tanks, then paused. Spraggue held his breath, willed them toward the door.

Instead, they started to climb, steadily, inexorably, creaking ever closer.

25

SPRAGGUE PRESSED DEEPER INTO THE CREVICE BETWEEN two stacks of barrels and held his breath. He fought the impulse and forced himself to inhale while he peered through the mountain of barrels, straining to find a peephole that would give him a glimpse of the head of the stairs. The footsteps ascended regularly.

Spraggue drew a mental map of the huge room. Plenty of hiding places: behind the barrels, under the tarp, in shadowy corners. But only one way out: the stairs. There must have been another window once, a double window dating from the days when the winemaker's art needed the assistance of gravity, when the grapes would have been hauled up to the second and third floors of the old stucco building. Spraggue remembered pictures in books of the cranes leaning out of the huge windows. He stared at the wall behind him, realized that the ornamental framing was just a blind. The windows had been boarded over long ago. He pried at the edge of a plank with his fingers. Sound, strong slabs of wood. No way out.

He glued his eye to a likely crack between barrels and

saw a cone of artificial light appear on a corner of the landing. He no longer needed to keep his eye focused on the spot to learn the identity of Lenny's killer; he kept it there in the faint hope that the beam issued from the flashlight of some law-enforcement official.

A familiar face and then a rotund body made their way into his field of vision. Philip Leider stood on the top step. The flashlight in his left hand outlined the gun clasped in his right.

Well, old Harry Bascomb of *Still Waters* would surely have had a gun in a situation like this, Spraggue thought. Even when he'd been a bona fide private investigator, he'd never carried one. He didn't even like to think about cold steel cylinders and bits of flying metal and what the combination could do to fragile human skin and bone.

"You may as well come out, Spraggue." Leider's voice was low, but it easily filled the room.

It wasn't what Spraggue had expected. He cursed under his breath. Leider was playing it safe, not tricky. In Spraggue's preferred script, the winemaker would have sneakily pocketed the gun, called out his old friend, Michael, for a friendly chat about possible misunderstandings, and attacked when he'd spied the chance. Maybe Leider realized too well that the empty winery was a confession of guilt, that Spraggue was more than a match for him in close combat. The fat man was doing things right so far: commanding the only exit and keeping his gun ready to fire. Great.

Spraggue wondered how long they'd have to play standoff before Leider's flashlight battery failed. It was probably good for the night, and there was every reason to expect the sun to rise on the morrow, although he wouldn't necessarily be around to witness the event. Spraggue replayed his parting from Kate. "Stop off for a bottle of wine" was all he'd said. Nothing about Leider. So when Enright, infuriated, phoned Kate and demanded his whereabouts, she wouldn't know. Leider had infinite time for his cat-and-mouse game. No hope of the cavalry to the rescue. The cavalry was probably eagerly charging off in a totally different direction.

If he stayed quiet, would Phil assume that he'd gone up to the third level? Would Phil be dumb enough to climb one more flight and let him escape?

"I know you're here," Leider said. Spraggue heard a faint creak and, to his dismay, Phil settled himself on the second step leading up to the third floor, a perfect vantage point. Because the wooden steps had no risers, the vintner could, with a turn of his head, keep the whole room under surveillance while blocking off exit from either floor.

"You've got us both into quite a mess," Leider said conversationally. "Why not come out and talk about it?"

Why not? The corners of Spraggue's mouth twisted in a bitter smile as he framed a silent answer: one automatic pistol.

"Did Lenny come out when you called?" he asked.

Phil Leider stood abruptly. A slow smile spread over his wide face. "Lenny was a fool," he said. "A conceited ass. There he was, absolutely bleeding me dry, but when I begged him, ever so humbly, for his exalted opinion of my '80 Cabernet, he trotted right over like the proverbial lamb."

"Didn't he realize you weren't crushing this year? The smell—"

"Not until it was too late," Leider said. "I had everything prepared—the empty tank, a heavy stick . . . I had all the right pipes connected."

"Was Lenny conscious when you poured the wine in on top of him?" A pretty question; Spraggue wrinkled his mouth in distaste, but Leider seemed pleased by the opportunity to talk. And talk held off action. So talk, Spraggue thought bitterly. Do what an actor does best. Talk.

"Not at the beginning," Leider said calmly. "But the bastard knew what was in store for him at the end. When I opened the valves and the wine came rushing in, he knew. Practically skinned his fingers trying to crawl up the side of the tank. No fingerholds in those tanks, you know. Sheer sides, completely sheer."

While Leider spoke, Spraggue took inventory. He emptied each pocket in turn and itemized the contents. Right front pants pocket: keys to the distant car. Had Leider bothered to disable it? In an analogous situation, Spraggue knew that he would have removed the distributor cap before entering the winery. Would Leider have done the same? Change and a few crisp bills, a leather packet of credit cards, none apt to be overly useful again. Left front pants pocket: knife with various attachments, including corkscrew and pocket flash. The knife was an ornamental two inches long, not enough blade to frighten a child. Considering Leider's bulk, it was an almost futile weapon, one that would have to be aimed at the neck in order to hit a vital spot. And getting within reach of Leider's neck was a remote possibility as long as he clutched that gun.

Spraggue found Lenny's address book in his back pants pocket. The breast pocket of his shirt had an alligator on it and nothing inside.

The fat man peered cautiously around the room, did a slow spiraling search, then settled down to flash his beam through the barrel mountain's cracks. Spraggue crouched behind the lowest keg he could find. Sharp metal pressed against his ribs and he hastily withdrew the tape recorder from his last unexplored jacket pocket. He punched the record button and flicked it on, smothering the soft whirring noise in his shirt. It sounded like overhead aircraft, but Leider didn't seem to note anything amiss.

The machine recorded silence, broken by Spraggue's steady breathing. It wiped out all the carefully studied lines and cues from *Still Waters*. And what did that matter, Spraggue thought, when he wouldn't be around to recite them? If he could tape Leider's confession, hide the tape, at least— At least what? Where would he hide it? Who would think to look? If his body was found afloat in a vat of Pinot Noir, would the acid have eaten away the cassette? What he needed was an escape plan, not a recording.

"Why don't you tell me the gory details, Phil?" he said.

178

For now, keep Phil talking, keep him from doing something irrevocable. "All about Mark Jason. Then maybe I'll come out."

Leider laughed. Hell, Leider ought to feel comfortable enough to laugh; he was holding all the cards. "A fairy tale?" he said. "Before you go to sleep?"

"A horror story," Spraggue said, hoping the recorder was picking up both sides. "About a berserk winemaker."

"I don't know that one. How about the 'Three Little Pigs'?"

"I'll prompt," Spraggue offered. "I know almost every line."

"Bragging?"

"Maybe. Check it out. Aren't you curious?"

"Not particularly."

"When did you first decide to sell the winery?" Spraggue asked.

"Come out where I can see you."

"Come in after me."

"Go ahead and tell your horror story," Leider said.

Spraggue inched over to a new barrel, peered through the crack. Leider wanted to keep him talking, too, so he could pin down the sound. Great. With each of them trying to get the other to talk, he might have a long-playing album on his hands.

"Once upon a time," Spraggue found himself saying in a nursery-calm voice. The "Three Little Pigs" reference must have stuck in his mind. "—There was a big fat piggy who got fed up with the wine industry."

"No crime in that."

"He mismanaged his winery," Spraggue said, "blew all the cash that should have gone into upkeep and repairs on fancy cars and a monstrosity of a house."

"You don't like my taste," Leider said. "Pity."

Spraggue stared up at the wall of barrels in front of him. The wood-frame barrel rack resembled a jungle gym. Spraggue considered the similarity. His eyes narrowed. He tucked the tape recorder back into his jacket pocket, shifted his weight to his left foot, untied one shoe.

179

"Keep talking," Leider demanded.

"Well, this ingenious swine doped out a plan to sky-rocket the net worth of his winery before offering it to a corporate hog. United Circle, right?" The floor was cool under Spraggue's stockinged feet. He shoved one shoe under his arm, abandoned the other.

Leider chuckled as the flashbeam pried closer. "How on earth did he manage that, the clever pig?"

Spraggue placed one foot on the wooden barrel rack, tested the strength of the supports. "Why, he decided some of his swill would look better in classier bottles. Bottles labeled 1975 Cabernet Sauvignon, Private Reserve." The rack was solid. Spraggue half-zipped his jacket, stuffed the shoe inside, and started to climb.

"What a smart piggy," Leider said. "That wine was bottled gold."

"How much a bottle?"

"Retailers are getting over thirty-five dollars. It went on the market for seven."

Spraggue switched back to his nursery-tale voice. "Now the piggy planned to be long gone with the cash before anyone bitched about the inventory."

"Are you kidding, Spraggue? That was the beauty of it. No one would have had the nerve to complain. After I copped the '79 Académie tasting, you wouldn't believe the requests I got for that stuff. Not from the regular places, from goddamned corner liquor stores in Oshkosh. From shops that just wanted prestige labels on their shelves. From the airlines, for Christ's sake!"

"I tried a bottle on TWA," Spraggue said.

"Damn them! They had specific instructions to age it another year."

"I assumed they'd stored it wrong."

"See?" Leider was clearly delighted. "If anyone with half a palate did taste a spurious bottle, he'd blame it on storage."

Spraggue clung to the rack and inhaled deeply. If he started gasping for breath, if the strain of the climb showed in his voice, Leider might catch on.

"Go on with your story," Leider said expansively. "I'm beginning to enjoy it."

Spraggue murmured a silent prayer and swung himself over the topmost barrel. From ten feet up, he could just see Leider, revolving like a plump top near the landing, uncertain where the voice in the dark originated. The gun glinted in the flashbeam. Harry Bascomb would have known what make it was.

"Go on," Leider ordered. "Talk."

"But the piggy needed to blend his swill." Spraggue was pleased with the sound of his voice. No gasping, no quavers. "He didn't want it to taste all that different from Lenny's prize-winning '75, at least not at first. So he hired an innocent student from U.C.–Davis. That was around Christmastime, wasn't it, Phil?"

"Mark Jason was all in favor of playing a joke on the wine snobs."

"But I'll bet he didn't know you were planning to sell out to United Circle. If Lenny hadn't spilled the—"

"Damn Lenny," Leider muttered, much too softly for the recorder to pick up.

"If it hadn't been for Lenny," Spraggue continued, "your whole scam might have worked."

"It'll still work!" Leider screamed the words, and Spraggue, staring down from the mountaintop, could see the sickly color in his fat face, the beads of sweat on his brow. Maybe murder wasn't so easy for him after all. Or perhaps the dull flush that spread across his cheeks was primed by fear, terror at the details Spraggue already knew. Maybe Phil imagined that Spraggue had told others....

"How did Lenny find out? Did he realize you were getting rid of him when you sent him over to Holloway Hills?"

"Never," Leider said. "I maneuvered it nicely, made him think the move was his own idea, that I was heartbroken at the prospect of going on without him. He ate it up."

"Then how?"

181

"Lenny stole a case of wine, one crummy case. I'd given him his share when he left. But that wasn't enough for Lenny. He'd made it; he thought all the wine was his."

Spraggue, with the glimmering of a plan in his mind, struggled forward down the mountain of barrels an inch at a time. He was no longer in danger of exposure from the flashlight beam; the front edge of the barrel tower would have deflected the light had Leider thought to raise it so high. The chief peril now was a sudden fall. Spraggue tested each barrel before straddling it. Most were full, heavy, solid, and quiet. He said, "And Lenny must have donated a bottle from that special case of his to George Martinson. Rotten luck."

"Worse for Martinson than for me," Leider said. "The Leider Cabernet had an unassailable reputation by that time. And then that L.A. paper reviewed one of the original bottles. George Martinson was a laughing stock."

"Lenny threatened him," Spraggue said.

"Good."

"But then Lenny himself must have tried a bottle from the mislabeled case, right? And he went straight off to confront the guilty hog." As Spraggue spoke, his nursery-tale voice serene, he wiped the sweat off his forehead and sank back against a barrel. One slip and he was gone. If the fall didn't kill him outright, Leider would hardly miss an unconscious target. Spraggue wondered idly if the fat man was strong enought to lift him, if he had another tank prepared, a few leftover sulfur sticks.

"Dammit, Spraggue," Leider shouted. "I thought Lenny would see it the way I did. As a joke on a conglomerate, on all those wine snobs who can only tell what they're drinking by the label and the price."

"How did Lenny see it?" Spraggue led Leider on while surveying the barrel mountain, searching for the key location.

"He didn't want me to sell. Or if I did sell, he wanted to buy. A song down, forever to pay."

"Not quite your intention."

"It was blackmail!"

182

"So . . ." Spraggue found a barrel formation that would do, started carefully toward it. "You paid him off for a while. You probably even let Lenny use certain locations in your new house for his obscene amateur photography."

"How did you—"

"He stowed the negatives in the cellar at Holloway Hills."

"You see what kind of vermin the man was? You could line up the people who wanted Lenny dead, just the *women* who wanted him dead, and get a line from here to—"

"From here to the county jail, Phil."

"Enough, Spraggue. The steps are the only way out and—"

"But I'm getting to the best part," Spraggue protested.

"I didn't want to kill Lenny." Spraggue couldn't see Leider's face, but he bet the man was drenched in perspiration by now.

"He forced my hand," Leider said. "Money wasn't good enough for him anymore. He decided his reputation was in jeopardy. His *reputation*! You'd have thought *his* name was on the bottle, not mine! He was going to turn me in so his goddamned *reputation* wouldn't get sullied. Send me to prison, screw the deal with United Circle."

The triad of barrels Spraggue had spotted looked perfect, slightly unstable with a wide enough depression behind a key barrel for Spraggue to fold himself into the slot. Even if he couldn't manage to kick the right barrel loose, he'd be out of sight, safe from all but the luckiest of shots. Spraggue wasted a minute staring down the hole, wondering if he'd be able to squirm his way out. Maybe not; maybe he'd starve to death, and next spring, when the United Circle vintner made his rounds to top off the barrels, he'd find a corpse clutching a tape recording.

"So you had to kill Lenny." Spraggue used the words to prod Leider to further defense. He didn't want any long periods of silence now.

"Not then," Leider corrected. "I laughed in his face. He didn't have a smidgen of proof. A case of wine was mislabeled. Tough. Someone made a mistake."

"When did Lenny locate Mark Jason?"

Leider's toes tapped the wooden floor. His voice bit off the brittle words. "He knew I'd have needed help. I couldn't blend the wine myself, couldn't run the damn bottling line alone. Once he found Jason, he had to die. They both had to die."

The top barrel of Spraggue's chosen triad was blessedly empty. One of the other two seemed only partially full. Spraggue crawled down into the crevice. If he executed the maneuver just right, he might start an avalanche of barrels.

"Is that the end of your story?" Leider asked, his voice back in control. "Isn't the big bad pig supposed to get punished? Or was he too clever for you?"

Spraggue wriggled over on his back, drew his knees up to his chest, and pressed his feet flat against the key barrel.

"Spraggue, say something!"

With last-minute inspiration, Spraggue fumbled the shoe out of his jacket pocket. If he could create a loud noise, far away, Leider might help him out by taking a few steps away from the precious landing. He took a deep breath and flung the shoe hard over his head. It smacked satisfyingly against the far wall.

The flashbeam jerked. Leider took three quick steps forward. The silence, the tension, the sudden noise betrayed him. He fired his gun wildly, in the direction of the fallen shoe. Spraggue closed his eyes and put every muscle he commanded into the task of straightening his bent knees.

The room exploded with barrels and bullets. Spraggue jumped for the landing.

"You missed." Barely halfway down the flight of stairs, Spraggue heard the hissing whisper and whipped his head around. Leider, on the landing, raised his pistol steadily. It had a bore as big as a cannon's mouth.

Without conscious thought, Spraggue fell.

26

THE STUNTMAN'S WORDS ROARED IN HIS HEAD: RELAX, cradle your head, hit with your thighs. Leider's gun barked. The fall took forever, like a slow-motion replay of one of the Boston location shots.

Roll when you land! His ankle ached and his breath came in sharp, painful jabs but he kept moving, veering in and out between the tanks. He tried the steps to the catwalk; his ankle refused the climb. He passed the centrifuge, spotted the switch, and flicked it on. Machinery droned. Everything he passed, he switched on, hiding his dragging, panicked footsteps in a forest of noise. The bladder press wheezed. The bottling line rattled through its empty motions. Every door he tried was locked. The windows were too high for escape.

Moonlight filtered through the dusty panes. Sp8ague was shocked by the darkness. He had no sense of the time spent on the second floor; it could have been three minutes or three hours. Surely, by now, someone would be searching for him. Someone might find those broken bottles at Lenny's place, figure out where he'd gone and why. . . .

Behind a huge wooden tank, Spraggue collapsed on the floor and rubbed his swelling foot.

The roaring machinery benefited the hunter as well as the hunted. Leider couldn't hear Spraggue's rasping breath. Spraggue strained for Leider's approaching footfalls.

The bottling line jerked to a halt. The bladder press gasped and gave up. Leider turned off the centrifuge. His footsteps rang on the catwalk steps. "You didn't finish your story," he said. The flashlight made him a moving target. But he had the only gun.

Dammit. Leider had a strategic position overlooking the room. Leider had the keys. Leider had the gun. How many bullets did the fat man have left?

Spraggue ran a hand through his hair, clamped his lips together. Shit. Old Harry Bascomb would know. Given a single split-second glance at Leider's hunk of blue-gray metal, he'd ID it as a .38 caliber Webley or whatever automatic. He'd holler, "That's your final shot, Leider. Your number's up!" Or some such garbage.

Spraggue was almost certain, he'd heard four distinct shots at the top of the stairs. And three on the way down. Seven. . . . That seemed about right for an automatic. But he couldn't be sure.

In answer to his unspoken question, he heard a sound that could only be a magazine clicking home in Leider's pistol. Seven more shots. How could he draw them without playing clay pigeon? Did Leider carry yet another clip?

The catwalk creaked overhead, and Spraggue scuttled crablike around to the other side of the tank.

"Why the hell . . . couldn't you just . . . leave me alone?" Leider shouted. His breath came in great gulps, tearing the sentence into three separate bits. His agitation and grief were palpable. He was starting to fray, his self-possession coming apart at the seams. Spraggue hoped his emotions would affect his marksmanship.

186

"Why did you try to pin it on Kate?" Spraggue asked. Leider whirled and fired. Three shots lodged themselves harmlessly in the tank. Spraggue waited for a fourth, but none came. Leider must have pulled himself together, realized the folly of firing with no clear target. Three shots gone.

"I had to," Leider said. Spraggue held up the tape recorder and shook it. It whirred merrily along. During the fall, his ribs had sustained more damage than the machine.

"Everyone said that Kate would sell out," Leider continued. "Some executive from United Circle was sniffing around Holloway Hills. Dammit, I'd spent most of a year negotiating with them. If they'd bought Holloway Hills, that would have killed my deal. Holloway Hills has a better location, better facilities."

"Kate would never have sold," Spraggue said.

"I'm supposed to take that on faith? I had to dump the bodies; I thought I'd put Kate out of action at the same time. She couldn't sign any United Circle contract from a jail cell."

"What a very clever piggy you are," Spraggue said. "Only—"

"Only you had to stick your nose in. And keep it in, even after I got Kate off the hook. Why the hell couldn't you . . ."

Spraggue felt a deep sick wrenching in his gut. That was why a teenager had been found in the trunk of an abandoned car so far from Holloway Hills. . . .

"You murdered that boy just to get me off your back," he said haltingly, hoping for Leider's denial.

"You were starting to be a greater risk than the chance of Kate selling out to United Circle." Leider laughed softly, a laugh tainted by a hint of hysteria. "Don't you remember what I told you coming down in the car that first day? Hitchhikers gamble every time they get in a car with a stranger." The vintner's laugh intensified.

"You're crazy," Spraggue said. He spat into a corner and forced himself to think—not about some child killed

187

without compunction—but about how to take this Leider, this sweating, giggling maniac. How to wrap his hand around that fat throat...

"On the contrary," Leider hollered triumphantly. "I considered the matter carefully. Judiciously. A third 'Car-Trunk' slaying would make even the most moronic cop release Kate. The murder was a refinement, another step in an unavoidable chain of regrettable actions. My sole error was in figuring that you would drop the whole mess and return to work you're more suited for."

Spraggue liked the way Leider's voice had tightened when he'd called him crazy. He picked at the sore. "You loony bastard," he said. "You psycho case—"

"I'm a pragmatist," Leider shouted. "I did exactly what I had to do, no more, no less. Every act was well planned. A reason behind every act."

"Why did you use sulfur dioxide on Mark Jason? You could have drowned him, too, couldn't you? But the cruelty appealed to you, turned you on." Spraggue put all the disgust he hadn't been able to spit out into his voice.

"Shut up! Come out where I can see you. If you do, I'll give you an easy death, a clean death. Later, I might change my mind, shoot you in the kneecap first—"

"Was setting fire to Jason's apartment carefully planned?" Spraggue said quickly. Bringing out the worst in Leider wouldn't help if he gave the vintner a chance to think, to plan instead of react. "You could have killed twenty, thirty innocent people."

"How was I to know what papers Jason might have kept, linking him to me? You forced my hand that time, too; I never thought you'd get that far. Even when I overheard you say you were going up to Davis, I never dreamed. But when I saw you hurry out of his apartment, hurry out empty-handed, I had to act quickly. I improvised. That's where most criminals fail. They have no imagination, and they're not willing to take the necessary steps. I'm different. I'm special. Don't think I'll hesitate to kill you."

Full-blown megalomania, Spraggue thought. With God knows what kind of delusions.

"Hey, Phil," he said in a stage whisper. "Have you been listening to yourself lately? Giggling and gibbering. Out of control. I doubt you could stop killing if you wanted to. After me, who? You want the list of everybody else who might be on to you?"

"Who knows?" Leider screamed.

"Or maybe you'd rather tell me about that boy you killed. . . . Why would Enright call that a sex murder?"

"That was part of the plan," Phil said defiantly. "They'd know it wasn't Kate Holloway, wasn't a woman."

"But they already knew it couldn't be Kate. She was in jail, Phil. Remember? What kind of movies do you show at your house, Phil? Family-night stuff? Did you help Lenny out with his photography?"

The bullet's ricochet came closer than Spraggue liked, but he was certain he'd found another wound to probe. Four bullets gone.

"You read about those crazy perverts, Phil? What happens to them when they get caught? Tough life in the state prison. The guards won't dare put you in with the general population because of what they'd do to you, Phil."

"Shut up! You hear me? Shut up!"

Spraggue's fingers worked at his key ring. He removed the corkscrew and tossed it against a distant steel tank. Leider whirled and fired twice. Six shots gone. Was that enough? The uniformed Boston police, he knew, carried the S&W six-shot revolver. Had he actually heard seven shots before Leider changed the clip? Had his imagination or an echo played him false?

"Bad shot, loony," he yelled. "Why don't you tell me about the boy? About what you did before you strangled him? Did you bring him here, Phil?" What else could he throw? Not the car keys. If Leider hadn't put the station wagon out of commission, he'd need it. If he got away. He hurled his tiny flashlight in the opposite direction and again it drew fire.

Where the hell was old Harry Bascomb when you

needed him? *If* he'd counted right, *if* the pistol held seven slugs, then Leider was either out of ammunition or inserting a fresh magazine. Spraggue decided not to take any chances.

He let out a heartrending groan, just the kind of sound Dave, the actor, made when he died on the trolley tracks at Park Street Station.

The catwalk swayed. Leider hurried over to the tank he'd fired upon a moment ago, his flashbeam searching for Spraggue's prostrate body. Spraggue was shocked by the man's appearance. Saliva dripped from one corner of his open mouth. His face was a livid, chalky white.

Spraggue shut off the tape recorder, removed the cassette, jammed it into a niche under the tank. He hefted the now empty tape recorder, measured the distance between himself and the outline of Leider's belly. He was almost close enough, but only a major league catcher could make a throw like that from his knees.

Supporting his weight against the tank, Spraggue straightened up, aimed at the light, heaved the recorder up and to the right, dead on target.

Leider saw it coming late, sidestepped, flailed wildly. Spraggue hit the floor, just in case the fat man had managed to reload.

Leider stumbled, tottered against the flimsy rotten guardrail. Screamed.

For an instant, Spraggue thought Leider might regain his balance.

He plummeted awkwardly, landed with a sickening thud, one leg at a horribly unnatural angle, his gun arm trapped under his massive chest.

As Spraggue scrambled to a sitting position, a blaring voice filled the room: Bradley's voice, dehumanized, amplified a thousand times.

"Come out with your hands up," the deputy cried.

Leider, a twisted mass on the wooden floor, groaned softly, struggled to move, failed.

By the time the cops found Spraggue, he was twisting

his shirt around his swollen ankle, laughing to himself. "Come out with your hands up!" he repeated delightedly. Maybe the dialogue in *Still Waters* was better than he'd thought.

27

"TEN MINUTES!" SHRIEKED THE ELEGANTLY TANNED production assistant, a brightly garbed blonde whose enthusiasm proclaimed her a novice. Spraggue tried not to limp as he walked wearily off the set. He pulled the letter out of his pocket, slit the envelope with Harry Bascomb's nasty little prop-knife. Settling himself gingerly in a softly upholstered chair, he rested his bandaged ankle on a stool. "Keep off that foot as much as possible," the doctor had warned. Sure.

He rubbed a hand across his forehead. The pressures of playing tough guy with three cracked ribs, a sprained ankle, and assorted bruised and tender spots all over his body were starting to get him down. The taped ribs itched like crazy. He stifled the impulse to scratch. Hell, old Harry Bascomb would have taken those steps with hardly a scrape off his hard-boiled flesh.

The envelope was square, marked "Photos—Do Not Bend."

"Michael, dear." Kate's inverted greeting was as standard as her spiky printing and her purple-ink-on-lavender-stationery combination. Her correspondence needed no signature, much less a return address.

Well, Howard's agreed to come back, [the letter began]. I'm giving him a raise. He didn't ask for one; he wouldn't. But I'm sure you'll agree that he deserves one in his own convoluted way. If he hadn't *finally* gone to the cops with those pages from Lenny's cellar book, I shudder to think what might have happened to you...

God, Howard must have been *furious* when I hired Lenny! Imagine our bumbling Howard actually breaking into Lenny's place, bent on revenge! And, finding no one home, *stealing* those pages from Lenny's cellar book!

Of course, the more I brood on it, the more likely it seems. Howard just wanted to improve himself by studying Lenny's secrets. (I *will* try not to tell him that it was *never* his wine-making skill that I doubted, just his personality that I *can't stand*. Tactful of me, don't you think?)

Wasn't it *brave* of Howard to go to the police? Belatedly brave, I'll admit. But then he thought he'd get thrown in the clink himself, for stealing Lenny's book. Besides, it took him a while to figure out Lenny's added notes on Leider's '75 Private Reserve. (And a while longer to get up his nerve. Thank God, he had enough sense to go straight to Bradley. Enright would have terrified him to death.) Anyway, Howard's timing certainly worked out well for you. But then you always had the luck.

Your tape recording turned out to be a gem. You, of course, came through loud and clear; Leider's voice is very faint, but definitely understandable. His attorney is making "inadmissible evidence" noises, but no one pays him any mind.

One sad thing: I did as you asked, hung around

and played mother hen when Carol Lawton came up to identify her Mark. Poor kid . . . She went back to stay with her parents. She's young. But I wonder if you can ever get over something like that . . .

Spraggue, about those photos . . . A confession: I haven't turned them over to the police. Mostly because I'd hate to corrupt Enright's beastly mind any further. I mean, I can't stand half those women, but I just *can't* turn the stuff in. Lenny was a worse toad than I thought.

Mary Ellen Martinson was well represented. (Well endowed, too.) She must have been looking for Lenny's dirty picture collection when she called on Grady. Further confession: I burned the photos and the negatives. So that you won't just have to take my word for the artistry involved, I've sent you one sample—of a lady who I'm sure wouldn't mind.

So all's well, et cetera, darling. My "Mr. Baxter" is fine, but I have that "he's going-back-to-his-wife-for-the-children's-sake" feeling. The crush is slowly winding down. Both Howard and I have hopes of an outstanding vintage.

Oh, I bought you a present. An entire case of Leider's '75 Private Reserve Cabernet. The real McCoy. According to George Martinson, it'll drink superbly around the year 2000. Imagine: you'll be fifty-three, with just a touch of gray at your temples; I, a mere child of fifty-one. Do you suppose we'll be settled, solid citizens at the turn of the century, our children already in their teens? Will a dignified middle age creep up on us or will we fall into bed exhausted after one more rip-roaring battle? Do you suppose those mythical children might be ours, yours and mine?

There was a sloping capital *K* for a signature, another Holloway trademark. And a postscript.

This should cheer you up: Enright was absolutely furious that Bradley made the arrest. A promotion is definitely in order. Don't you think Brad is a *very* attractive man?

Spraggue crumpled the note.

The envelope was stiff. He pulled out a thin packet, wrapped in brown paper, glanced fleetingly around the room: No one was watching.

No trouble identifying the model, even though the black-and-white print didn't do justice to that hair. The background clicked only after the first few minutes: that deep maroon sofa, the fat gray cushions . . . Part of the blackmail: Lenny got to use Leider's house for his off-beat entertainment.

Spraggue thought back to the evening of Leider's tasting, to Grady's blatant overtures in that same room. Had Phil been behind a camera, waiting to click some blackmail shots of his own? Had Grady known, been instructed? Was that the reason for her abrupt amorousness?

The sudden hum in the air told him a presence had entered even before the heavy steel doors banged shut. A head honcho; the whispers swelled like a spring breeze. The producer, maybe. Spraggue struggled to his feet.

Dear Lord.

Spraggue stared down at the nude photo, up at the clothed original.

She'd sure dressed for the occasion. Her jeans were the narrowest he'd seen in a city full of fashion-conscious asses. The pale pink shirt, frilled at the wrists, slit almost to the waist, did wonders—not the least of which was that it set that incredible hair on fire. Spraggue's mouth shaped itself automatically into a whistle-O.

Grady posed on her stilt heels, did a great bewildered look-around, murmured into an entranced focus puller's ear.

The poor guy hung on her words as if he were tuned into the last out of the last game of the World Series, turned and pointed in Spraggue's direction. Spraggue shoved the photo quickly in his pocket, got a welcoming smile together on his face. The director was already hurrying over, prancing, practically drooling.

"Michael!" Grady's voice was great, too: warm and low and sexy as hell. "I finally found you." Spraggue held back on the applause, but what an audition! He bit down hard on the inside of his cheek. Everod panted for an introduction.

A ripped-up ankle, itchy ribs, lousy scripts, and now Grady Fairfield, future star! Kate was right, he had all the luck.

"Places!" screamed the production assistant. Spraggue smiled down at Grady, saw her stretched out on Leider's sofa, barely wearing that soft green dress.... Had she been following Leider's orders? Posing for one of Lenny's hidden cameras?

He decided to give her the benefit of the doubt.

CLASSIC
JAMES
MICHENER